"Ready? Ready for what?" In the darkness, her eyes were wide but blind, her body shaking but immobile. "Ready for what, Greg?"

He was removing his shirt now, the sequel to his uniform pants and the most telling evidence of all. He tucked the dog tags into the pocket, then added his wallet for good measure. The shirt was folded neatly and placed at the very back of the cave, then covered with a rock. He returned to her, no longer sweet, funny Greg with the careless hair, but officer Greg, all business and brevity.

"If they come here, if they find us, we can't let them know that I'm a pilot, okay? Not one word of planes, pilots, military, officers, nothing. You understand."

She nodded, realized that he couldn't see it, then said, "Yes."

"We are a couple. Dating. We left Hawaii for a day on our boat out there and got caught in a storm and ended up here."

"Where? We don't know where we are. Hawaii could be on the other side of the world."

"I'm going with the greatest probability here." He swallowed loudly enough that she could hear it. "So, we're civilians who got trapped here after our boat got caught in a storm. We don't know anything about planes or the war or anything. I own my own garage in Fairbury, Nebraska, and you work at the library."

"Greg, I'm so scared."

Rendezvous Press is an imprint of Crossroad Press.

Cover by Dave Dodd
Design by Aaron Rosenberg
ISBN 978-1-937530-93-8 — ISBN 978-1-937530-94-5 (pbk.)
 For information address Crossroad Press at 141 Brayden Dr., Hertford, NC 27944
www.crossroadpress.com

First edition

Love Lost

Patricia Lee Macomber

CHAPTER ONE

The sun shimmered through dusty panes of glass, flashing off the requisite metal napkin holder and momentarily blinding Amanda. The tray tilted, shook. A tall glass of iced tea held its ground for a few moments, then tottered enough to slop tea onto the table in a generous puddle.

"Damn!" she spat out loud before she could catch herself.

She let the tray clatter to the table loudly, a rain of peas slipping over the edge of the institutional plate and rolling about aimlessly. There was tea on the tray, tea on the table, tea all over her hand. She snatched a wad of napkins from that guilty holder and began blotting at the mess furiously, cursing under her breath all the while. Her face red, hazel eyes flashing to crimson, she tore at the napkins, trying fruitlessly to wipe the sticky sweet tea from her hand.

She felt the burning gaze of a dozen pairs of eyes on the back of her neck. The soft hairs rose and prickled. Finally, she dropped into the chair and hung her head. Her taste for tea had waned, her appetite gone. For the briefest of moments, she was that small girl back in the cafeteria of PS42, sitting alone, mocked by nearly everyone and weeping into her Partridge Family lunch box. Amanda Stevens was about to cry.

"Having one of THOSE days, are we?"

Amanda's eyes shot upward, falling upon a smile which was brighter than it had any right to be. "Having one of those lives." She waved her hand in the general direction of the other chair and sighed. "Better not sit too close. It could be contagious."

Ignoring the fringe of acid on Amanda's words, Dana sat down, smoothing out her flowered skirt with great care and slipping her chin into the bowl of her cupped hands. "So, you had a little mishap.

Happens to us all. No need to get . . ."

"Oh, it's not that! Face it! I'm a mess!" Amanda ran her hands through her stringy blonde hair and bit into her lip. "My house is a mess. My yard is a mess. The boat is a mess. I have more work on my desk than I can get to in three lifetimes. Face it. I'm a bona fide disaster."

"You need to get away from things for a while. Take a vacation. Relax." Dana smiled again, this time a bit cooler. To Amanda she seemed bored, tired, probably, of hearing another in the long list of Amanda disasters.

"I tried to take a vacation once. Don't you remember? A simple drive up into the mountains to stay at a nice cabin and unwind. Halfway there, my car broke down. I went to call the auto club and by the time I got back, the road had iced up and my car had slid into a ravine."

Dana made a sour face and blinked. "Oh yea. I forgot about that one."

"I didn't." Amanda picked up her fork and pushed a few errant peas back into the communal pile, then made as if to eat them.

Dana sat back, folding her arms over her chest and watching as though she expected a light bulb to appear over Amanda's head. "You know what you need? You need a MAN."

Amanda laughed at that, the sound of it attracting more attention than her previous racket. "You HAVE to be kidding. We've been best friends for twelve years. In all that time, have you EVER known me to have a decent relationship?"

"Yes. Once." That pointed glare made shivers run up and down Dana's spine, but she forged on. "And you have to stop dwelling on it."

"Some people were made to be in relationships. And some people were made to be alone. I'm an alone kinda gal. And I've made my peace with that." She reached for the tea, suddenly drawing back her hand as though she'd been bitten. "Besides, I'm getting tired of hearing every man on the planet explain how I'm too detached to get serious about."

Dana reached out and grabbed Amanda's hand, yanking it to the center of the table. "Do you see how hard and rough and callused that hand is? And you hardly ever do any actual labor." She stretched across the table, stabbing at Amanda's chest with the same bony finger. "You mark my words, Mandy. If you don't learn to use it, your heart's gonna end up the same way."

Dana shoved back her chair and stood up from it, her heels drowning out the scrape of light metal against cheap tile. Amanda stared over her shoulder after her friend, jaw drooping and eyes wide. Was that all a callous act, meant for effect? Or was Dana really about to abandon her? For several very slow heartbeats, Amanda was very scared. Then her mouth shut, and her head turned, and the walls went up again.

In a small square of light cast by a small square screen, Amanda sat motionless. Her shimmering hazel eyes were captured by the visions in that television, visions that mocked her own memory and stalked her like time-traveling demons. The faces were familiar, owned and operated by the movie channel. The story was as old as time, more painful than death and twice as frightful.

As the heroine bent to kiss the life from her lover's lips, Amanda pulled a sour face. Her fingers were so tightly wrapped around the remote that the white of her knuckles glared through the darkness. Before the hero could die, before her own heart could release its tears, Amanda clicked the "off" button viciously and tossed the remote to the floor.

"Damn!" she cursed and launched herself from the chair.

Thin hands rubbed thinner-still arms as she tried to ward off the chill of that moment. It was too close, too familiar, too much her own pain. The people on that screen might as well have been Scott and her. He had died the same way, encased in white sheets and moaning through the agony of a life too full of suffering. The accident had been swift, but the suffering had drawn out for days. In the end, Scott gave up the fight. The pain of sorrowful life wasn't worth fighting to hold onto. Amanda wasn't worth living for.

Amanda shook her head violently, fighting to dislodge those memories before they could seep into her soul again. Enough sleepless nights and haunting half-remembered dreams. Life should go on, she thought, not stagnate and wither.

She wandered the house, searching in vain for something to distract her from those memories. If she tried to sleep now, the dreams would come and then the downward spiral would begin.

She'd been watching her feet, the way the little pink satin slippers slid and shuffled over the carpet. As she looked up, the hallway stretched out before her, impossibly long and growing longer with each passing second. At the end of it . . . the door. Not just any door, this was the door to her father's room. It was THE door, beyond which lay her father's things, his prized possessions, his soul. Everything he cared about was inside that room, everything save for the little boat which sat rotting at the dock for lack of use.

Amanda brushed back a lock of hair and leaned against the wall. The surface of it felt cool against her warm skin, lent some reality to that surreal moment. She chewed on her lip and straightened her back as a flood of new memories took root in her mind.

Her father, too sweet for words, bringer of grape life savers and fixer of broken toys, had left a giant hole in her life when he'd passed. In her mind's eye, she could see him returning from work, his overalls drenched in sweat and dusted with the metal shavings which had no doubt contributed to his early demise. But no matter how hard the day or heavy the load, he had always had a spring in his step, a gift in his pocket. Daddies never forgot their little girls and little girls never stopped worshipping their daddies.

Now she was an orphan, her father three years gone, and her mother dead from the moment of her birth. If everything had worked as she'd planned it, Scott would have been there to hold her up during those hard times. But like her parents and everyone else she'd ever known, he, too, had gone on to heaven without her.

"Stop it," she muttered to herself, shoving off from the wall and making ready to turn.

She couldn't do it. For three years, she had let that door taunt her and prey on her mind. It was time to go in, to face reality and cleanse herself.

Hands fisted, she marched on that door, determined to open it in one gigantic show of courage. Between beginning and end of that hallway, her resolve melted, sliding from her in little bits until she was left, shaking and sweating, before that door.

"Don't bother Daddy when he's working, Pumpkin."

The voice of their housekeeper was so clear, so loud, that it might well have traveled across inches rather than years. Amanda sighed and let her chin rest on her chest. The doorknob came into clear view then, a giant staring eyeball in her mind.

Dangling from that knob, unmoving, was a small brass key ring. That, too, had been her father's. It held the keys to his world. House, boat, den and car . . . everything he loved could be laid bare with a turn of those keys. Also dangling from that ring was the small ceramic heart she had made him in summer camp. It was aged and crackled, but the emotion behind it burned brightly.

Amanda reached out one delicate hand, watching as it shook its way to the knob. Fingers uncurled, closing again as they found kinship with the cool metal of the key. One turn and it was all over.

She shut her eyes as the door creaked open, frightened of what she might see. No, that wasn't entirely correct. She was more frightened of what she would NOT see. Her father should still be sitting there, tinkering with dials and adjusting headsets, just as he had been every night for nearly twenty years.

There was only an empty chair to greet her. The cold reality of that slapped her hard in the face, sent her head spinning as her emotions spiraled out of control. Daddy was gone, never to return. The scent of his aftershave lingered still.

She took one step into the room, her left hand gripping the door frame with all its might. Fainting was not merely a possibility. It was a very real threat.

The small swivel chair, gleaned from a junk yard and recovered in gray wool, held court over the vast array of radios and transceivers which had been her father's life-long hobby. Amanda's eyes passed over that chair, leaping from seat to back as they fell on the indention left by her father's constant presence. From there, it was a short journey to the workbench which held his equipment.

Dust coated everything. A few homeless spiders had found sanctuary among the unused tools and parts. Their webs shimmered slightly in the half-light. They swung from the dials of the ham radio.

Amanda let out a little yelp and leaped to her feet, stunned by the fact that she had somehow slipped into that chair as she rode the wave of memories which had so suddenly washed over her. She could almost see her father's hand reaching for the dial. It brought tears to her eyes, sent them cascading over her cheeks in long rivers.

But it was only her own small hand which traced the rough edges of the dials, danced over the darkened meters and face plates. She knew nothing of her father's hobby. That had been his alone, something he had kept from her and had shared only with the disembodied voices halfway around the world.

Her wrist twitched and a meter glowed back to life with a moist pop of electricity. Amanda pressed one hand to her mouth, fingers twitching as they read the smile on her face. It worked. Somehow, everything still worked.

She studied the board for a moment, blinking rapidly as she marveled at her father's skill. He knew what every button and dial did. There was no need for labels. Amanda was lost among all that circuitry; helpless in the face of those knobs and buttons.

She tried the large knob, turning it carefully until something akin to a pig-squeal came out of the small box speaker. Static assaulted her ears, whisking away the squeal until there was nothing left of it. She turned it some more and heard silence. Another turn brought a faint hum, accompanied by the softest of voices.

"KG5 can you hear me?"

Amanda gasped and locked her hand tightly over her mouth. Before her, a large microphone sat, begging to be used. She stared at it, wide-eyed, hoping against hope that the other person wouldn't hear her. It felt like an intrusion to even be there, much less to be using her father's equipment to eavesdrop.

She spun the dial again, this time more briskly, listening as static and squawk melted into a dull roar. There, amid a high-pitched whistle, she found another voice.

". . . and I swear to God, that damn deer just ran off into. . . ."

She shook her head rapidly and turned the dial again, her face suddenly twisting into a mask of worry and confusion.

No sound. Silence. She pulled a face and reached out to the microphone button with one trembling finger. "Can anybody hear me?" Her voice, nearly as tremulous as her hands, sounded foreign to her.

There was no response.

"Hello?"

"I hear you just fine, little lady. I was eating a sandwich is all. Had my mouth full."

"Oh . . . hello." A smile sped onto her face, unbidden.

"Where you at, hon? What're your call letters?"

"Umm . . . I'm in Maine. What are call letters? You'll have to excuse me but I'm new to this." A few moments of dead silence reminded her to let up on the button.

". . . to identify yourself and your equipment."

"I'm not sure. This is my father's old radio. Where would I find those call letters?" She shifted in the chair, wiggling into her father's impression.

"Those should be on the mic somewhere. If not, they're probably pasted onto the front of the main receiver. That's where mine are at least."

"Oh. Oh!" She squinted at the large piece of masking tape on the front of the receiver and read slowly. "K-5-9-Z-Z-9."

There was a long pause, dead silence and the sudden fear that the equipment had stopped working. Amanda checked all the lights and found them still on. "Hello?"

"Sorry. But are you sure?"

"Yes, quite sure."

"You say that's your father's radio?"

"Yes, it is . . . or was. He's been dead nearly three years now."

"Well, that explains it then. Your father's name was Hal, right?"

Amanda slammed her back against the chair and stared at the microphone like it might attack. Slowly, her hand shaking even more than before, she leaned forward and pushed the button. "Yes."

"I used to talk to your dad every night. I'm up here at a weather station near Anchorage."

Tears choked off her words and stung at her eyes. Amanda coughed, trying to find her voice again. "Petey's gonna freeze up there."

"Say again?"

"That's what daddy used to say every morning over the newspaper. He'd read the weather reports and tell me, 'Petey's gonna freeze up there.' You're Petey, right?"

"Oh my Lord! You are Hal's little girl, aren't ya?"

"And you're his pal, Petey. He talked about you a lot. You were stationed in Anchorage eight years ago. And before that, you were at a Coast Guard station near Norfolk."

"I'll be danged!" She could hear the smile in the man's voice, across all those miles and through the static. Then it changed. "I'm real sorry to hear about your daddy. I tried getting in touch with him for about a year. Figured he had lost his license or maybe gotten sick. I sure am sorry he's gone."

"Tell me about my daddy. Please?"

Amanda awakened with a yelp, her head shooting up from the desk and twisting this way and that. The radio was still on, the lights mocking her with little waving indicators. Had she talked all night? When had she fallen asleep?

"Oh my God!" she groaned as she looked at her watch.

She turned off the equipment and bolted from the chair, gaining the middle of the hall before turning back to lock the door and hang the keys in their rightful place on the knob. Her father had always done it that way, and that's the way it should be done.

A quick shower and a piece of bread got her on her way, only a half hour late for work but enough to make her frantic. In all the years she'd worked at Barnes, she'd never once been late.

She drove like a madwoman, or as much like one as the old Chevy would allow. The nearly bald tires squealed into the parking space and she shoved open the door with one hand, even as the other was shutting off the engine.

Dana stared at her as she bolted past her desk. Her skirt whipped about her knees in the wind and her bag thumped her hip. She made quick work of putting away her things and turning on her computer, and then tried to catch her breath. It wasn't that Mr. Anderson would be mad at her for being late. She was mad at herself.

Dana approached, slowly and with a silly grin on her face. She grabbed Amanda's chin in one hand and turned her head to the left.

"So, what were you doing last night when you fell asleep?"

Amanda blinked stupidly. "Listening to the radio. Why?"

"Because you have the perfect imprint of a pen on your cheek." Dana laughed a bit and rested one hip on the desk.

Amanda produced a small mirror from her desk drawer and scrutinized her face. "Oh God!" She rubbed furiously at her cheek, trying to make the indentation go away.

"Must have been one hell of a radio show."

"Actually, I wasn't just listening to the radio. I was talking on it." Amanda looked up at her friend and offered a sheepish grin.

Dana's eyebrows shot up. "As in . . . the ham radio? As in . . . you went into your father's room? The room?"

Amanda bit into her lower lip and nodded curtly. "I met a man on the radio who used to be a friend of my dad's. They talked every night for like twenty years. He was telling me stories about my father."

Dana looked ready to pop off with one of her smart remarks. Then her face softened. "Well, that's really something, now isn't it? Very cool."

"Yes, it was. I didn't know my father wanted to be a writer. Petey did and he told me all about it."

Dana sported one of those smiles that told Amanda an argument would be forthcoming. "That's very special, sweetie. Now, if you happen to hook up with some handsome, rich, single radio jockey . . . I'll be two desks down."

Dana winked and left in a swirl of Patchouli and polyester.

Amanda sat back in her chair and rocked slowly, the smile taking over her face. She had spent most of the night talking to a man who lived thousands of miles away. And that man—a man who had never seen her father's face—had known her father better than she. It made her hungry for more.

Amanda dropped her things into the chair by the door and raced to the kitchen to grab a sandwich and a soda. She balanced the plate on top of the glass as she struggled to unlock the den door, and then set the whole load onto the desk beside the microphone.

She smiled as she turned on the radio, and then took a bite of the sandwich. It had been a long time since she'd had anything to look forward to. She hoped Petey was on already.

She flipped the switches and turned the knobs, listening to static and testing frequencies. Somewhere in that room was a stack of books about ham radios. She would have to read a few of them and learn what all the equipment did. Suddenly, she wanted that more than anything.

"Petey, are you there?" She leaned forward and listened intently, hoping for some sound. "Hello?"

The dial was exactly where she had left it the night before, and yet there was no sign of Petey.

She decided to try other frequencies. She wasn't sure, but she thought that people changed their frequency according to reception quality. She wasn't really sure about any of it.

She turned the dial and listened again, two men's voices breaking through the static. It was a private conversation, between a man and his son who had been stationed overseas. She turned the dial again.

". . . stupid carb is bad again and I don't know . . ."

There was a loud pop. It came from the receiver and sounded like a tube exploding. Amanda sat back and frowned, praying the radio still worked.

". . . .Rose, here to cheer, calling all you GI Joes to . . ."

Squawk! The tinkling woman's voice was cut off abruptly by another turn of that great dial. Amanda sighed and leaned forward, the rest of the room forgotten as she rested her elbows on the workbench and concentrated on the dial, searching for Petey.

"May day! May day!" Amanda sat back quickly, her jaw dropping open. "This is Alpha Tango Foxfire. Can anybody hear me?"

"Oh my!" Amanda gasped, both hands suddenly on her arms, rubbing away those goose bumps.

". . . taking on water . . . southern tip of the island . . . may day . . . may day . . . is anybody out there reading me?"

Amanda stabbed at the button on the microphone instinctively. She thought that's how her father had done it; hold down the button and speak, then let it up again.

"I can hear you. I'll get help. Where exactly are you?"

"May day! Alpha Tango Foxfire . . . one niner two . . . down . . . taking on water fast . . ."

"Can you hear me?" She was shouting now and very suddenly she didn't care. "Please! I can get you help but I need to know where you are." She let up on the button and frowned.

"That's a roger. I don't have . . . before the radio dies . . . southern tip of the island . . . you read?"

"What island?" No answer. Amanda shook so hard the chair beneath her rattled. "Tell me what island!"

"Send help, please! . . . can't let them take me!"

There WAS only one island. Prevatt Island. Amanda knew it well, had taken the boat out there a hundred times with her father. They had picnicked there, camped there. She couldn't imagine anything dangerous being near that island. Then again, she couldn't imagine things like car jackings or drug dealers either. The world was a scary place.

She left the radio on, spun in that chair and leaped for the doorway. She could reach that island in fifteen minutes, surely enough time to rescue this man before the waves took him.

Her hand was on her coat as the back door flew open. The keys were in the boat house, if only the motor would work. She had paid Mr. Ames to tend to the boat out of respect to her father. Now, she prayed that Mr. Ames was half as honest as he was smooth.

Outside, the wind wreaked havoc. It stirred the tree tops and tore at the shutters. Rain pelted her face and hands, forcing her raincoat to crawl up the back of her neck. It was a wretched night, even for the lower coast of Maine. It was no night to be out on the ocean in the dark.

Amanda bent her head low and charged toward the boat house. Her feet, still encased in soft pink satin, slipped and skittered across the dock. It was cold outside and wet, but surely she stood a better chance with bare feet than pink satin. Hopping a few steps, she cast off the offending slippers and hammered at the dock with bare feet.

Just inside the door, dangling precariously from a rusted hook, were the boat keys. She snatched them from their place and slammed the door, casting off the aft line as she hurried toward the boat's pilot house. Ideally, she would have someone with her who could cast off the bow line and haul in the fenders. But she didn't. So as not to lose the keys overboard, she slipped them into the ignition, then leapt to the deck and cast off the line.

Sailing with yer fenders hanging over the side is the mark of a sloppy seaman. Don't ever let me catch ye doing that, angel face. I'll have yer captain's license for that, I will!

"Fenders be damned!" she shouted into the wind moments before it tore the raincoat's hood from her head.

She turned the key and prayed, listening as the engine grunted and sputtered, trying to be heard above the roar of the wind and the steady kettle drum of the rain. She eased off and then turned it again, jerking it viciously to one side and praying. With a sudden spurt of energy, the motor roared into life and she slammed the boat into gear.

The boat lurched forward, the bow of it slicing into the wind as the inboard motor spat out noxious fumes and dark water. In moments, the boat was cutting through the water, the waves slamming against the hull as though they might rip it to shreds.

"Come on, come on!" she screamed, her teeth clenched so tightly she feared damage.

She kicked the thing into high gear, turning the wheel toward where she knew the island would be. So many journeys made exactly the same way. She could find the thing in the dark, blind, with one hand tied behind her back.

A darker shadow against a dark sky loomed before her, two miles out and closing fast. From the corner of one eye, she could see the buoy which marked the old wreck down below. She was right on target, determined not to stray. But then shadow changed to light, a huge wall of light ready to devour the boat and everything on it.

The thing was right at her bow by the time she saw it. It was tall and swirling with color, glowing with its own sort of light. It swallowed up the bow of the boat, drenching it first in color and then light, slowing the boat's progress as it did so.

Amanda had no time to react at first; that's how suddenly the thing had come upon her . . . or she upon it. One moment there had been nothing but blackness, the next, she was watching her father's beloved boat as the teeming mass of colors devoured it. Beyond the veil of light, she could see nothing of the ocean or the boat.

Time slowed. She watched her hand as it reached for the knob, begging it to hurry . . . hurry. That light, that THING, was almost upon her now. Inside her chest, her heart beat viciously, the blood thrumming in her ears and blotting out everything else.

Then it was as though she had hit some sort of wall. She felt her body make contact with it, though there was no pain in doing so. But it grabbed onto her as surely as if it had hands, and it shoved her backward.

Feet still firmly planted on the deck, her body slid backward, as stiff as though something was behind her, bracing her. The thing pushed at her, forced her backward as she screamed into the wind. Surely, she would be swept straight off the stern of the boat and into the water.

But when her legs made contact with the hull, her backward motion ceased. For a few terrifying seconds, boat, woman and light remained suspended, unmoving. And then, as though being born again, she was pressed through the light, shoved to the other side along with the boat.

Time resumed its normal function and Amanda fell forward, landing by the grace of God on both hands rather than her small nose. She was sobbing then, drenched in rain, sweat and tears, shaking hard enough to make her teeth chatter.

Every muscle in her body ached as if she had just run a marathon. For what seemed to her like an eternity, she lay on the deck of the boat, sobbing and shaking, praying that she would wake up from that dreadful nightmare.

Finally, she shoved off from the deck, casting a fearful glance over her shoulder at the path she had just taken. The light, the thing, the whatever-it-was . . . was gone. The boat's engine had stopped.

"Over here!"

Amanda screamed and spun to face the source of that urgent call. It was still night, still storming. But somehow, all was not as black as it had been moments before.

Ahead of her, some four hundred yards off the island and bobbing in the water like a fishing lure, stood the hulk of a wrecked plane. A lone man stood on its nose, waving both arms and yelling frantically.

She didn't think, couldn't think. Like a flash, she turned over that boat motor and set the thing in motion. It leaped forward like a prize mare and sped toward the drifting wreck.

CHAPTER TWO

Amanda shifted a bit and spat out sand. As her eyes fluttered open, the light stung them, forcing her to shut them again. Whatever she was lying on was hot and nearly fluid. It moved as she moved, tried to suck her down.

In a moment of panic, she shoved off from the surface, her eyes flapping open like broken shutters and her fingers digging into sand. The water was behind her, waves lapping at the shore and stealing back what they had left the night before.

She blinked and coughed. Her eyes and nose stung and her throat was raw. The last thing she remembered was the boat and the man. . . . "Hello?"

She sat back on her heels and looked around. Palm trees and blue sky greeted her, not exactly the usual Maine coast fare.

"Ah, you're awake."

Amanda screamed and leaped from the sand, pinwheeling her arms and staggering backward as she tried to spin and face the owner of that voice. "Who? Where are we? How did I . . . "

"I didn't mean to scare you." He set down the load of wood he'd been carrying and dusted off his hands. "Sorry. My name's Greg, by the way." He was the test-case for tall, dark and handsome, boyish grin and shimmering blue eyes included. His uniform, though a bit tattered and soiled from the ordeal, was neat in contrast to his stubbled jaw and wind-tossed hair.

"I'm Amanda and you didn't scare me." She lowered her eyes and focused on brushing the sand off her jeans, trying to avoid the man's gaze and her own shame as well. "How did I get here? The last thing I remember, I was on the boat and you were on top of the plane."

"That was one heck of a storm we had last night. Your boat took a hit from a large wave and you disappeared from sight. I figured you must have hit your head, so I jumped off the plane and swam over to your boat."

"But how did we get . . . here?" She looked around again, puzzled by the palm trees and the heat. Even at that time of year, the wind should be chilled and the sun partially veiled behind storm clouds.

"Your boat, of course. That was the strangest darn thing I've ever seen. All plastic and filled with dials and such. Where'd you get that thing, anyway?"

"It was my father's." She spun around and scanned the horizon for signs of the boat. "Where is it?"

"Over there." He pointed toward a large stand of trees and brush to her right. "Small aside. Did you know that this entire island is surrounded by rocks? Neither did I. I'm afraid your boat is a goner."

"Oh no! How bad is it?"

"The hole's pretty big, I'm afraid." His shoulders slumped and he studied his feet. "Hey, that's why I became a pilot instead of a sailor."

Amanda sighed and stared at the ground. "Where are we, anyway?"

"I'm not exactly sure. That will take some figuring. The way I see it, we must be on the Spratly Islands. I was headed for the Philippines when I crashed."

"That's impossible!"

"Oh yea? What makes you say that?" His tone was angry, but he smiled in spite of it.

"Because, when I went to rescue you, I left my house in Maine."

He stood for a moment, unmoving and stunned into silence. "Maine."

"Yes, Maine. And I was only in the boat for about fifteen minutes."

"Well, I didn't have nearly enough fuel to fly to Maine. So we can't be anywhere near there."

"And I didn't have the time or fuel to make it to the South Pacific. So we can't be anywhere near there."

"So . . ."

". . . where are we?"

They stared at each other for a few minutes, confusion setting in and fear taking root. Finally, Amanda turned to the man and frowned.

"Now I'm scared."

"Yea. Me too." More goose bumps arrived and she warded them off by rubbing her arms again. "Well, no matter where we are, we need to figure out how to get out of here. The boat may be wrecked, but the radio should still work."

She set off across the sand, bare feet nearly disappearing with each step. She didn't care if the man followed her or not. She just wanted to get her hands on that radio and call for help.

She twisted the knob and waited for that familiar staticky hum. A shadow fell over her shoulder and she glanced back at the man, her lip caught in the vice of her teeth.

"Looks like it's dead."

"Yea." She sighed and gave the knob another try. Nothing. "It's dead for sure." She turned and surveyed the horizon, squinting against the sun and frowning. "We could always build a signal fire. Somebody's bound to pass by and see it."

"No, ma'am. We don't want the wrong people seeing it."

"Wrong people?" She turned her glare on him and shook her head in confusion for a moment. Then she nodded. "Oh, yes. Drug dealers and such. You're right."

He nodded.

"Well, I guess there's nothing we can do but wait. Too bad we don't know how to make batteries out of coconuts."

"Excuse me?"

She laughed. "It works on TV."

"TV?" His face was near comical in its portrayal of confusion.

"You know . . . television? Little square box with pictures?"

"I guess I've been out of the states a little too long. I've lost touch with what's happening."

"Anyway, I guess we should find food and some sort of shelter. There must be some pineapples and coconuts around here someplace. Maybe even a banana tree."

"And fish. I reckon I could catch some fish."

"Okay, then. At least we have purpose now. Let's go grocery shopping, shall we?"

He offered up his first genuine smile and Amanda found it charming. He reminded her of Scott, with his boyish charm and the blazing blue eyes. She shook off the threat of bad memories and trudged across the sand once more.

The sun had begun to rise and so had the heat. Amanda swiped the sweat from her brow as she trudged through the thick growth of the island. It was nothing like Maine, either in climate or appearance. It was like one of those dreams she used to have where she was riding her bike through the neighborhood and suddenly couldn't recognize anything.

". . . coconuts but I don't have anything to open them with."

She blinked at him stupidly, only then realizing that he had been speaking for as long as they had been walking. She had heard none of it.

"That's a good point."

It's what she always said during a meeting when she wanted to make sure the boss knew she was listening but didn't want to offer up any real advice.

"You're a city girl, aren't you?" The breeze tossed an errant lock of hair over his brow and he swept it back with one tanned hand.

"I live in a small town, but I work in the city, yes. How did you guess?"

"The way you're walking along. Like nothing on earth could be out in these bushes but you and me." That smile again and she nearly melted from it.

"So what is in these bushes? Besides us, I mean?"

"Bananas."

She looked at him querulously and laughed. "Oh, like I should be afraid of bananas."

"No, I mean there's bananas right here."

She followed his arm with her gaze and smiled as she spotted the bright green banana tree with its huge cluster of large bananas. Without a second thought, she reached out her hand and grasped a banana.

His hand shot out and slapped hers away. "Bananas have banana spiders. Their bites hurt and it can make you sick." He scanned the ground for a stick, plucking it from the vines and dirt in a short sweeping motion. "You want to make sure those little buggers are out of there before you shove your hand in."

She stood by and watched as he beat the leaves of the tree and tapped at the banana bunch. Large brown legs reached out and bodies scurried over the tree fronds. It made Amanda shudder outwardly. Once he was sure they had all evacuated, he reached one well-muscled arm into the leaves and pulled out a banana.

She smiled as she took it from him, her hand brushing his for a moment and sending a warm shock up her arm. For just a moment, she allowed her eyes to meet his, and then turned to the task of peeling the banana, lowering her eyes and head to avoid the blush that had already heated the fringes of her face.

"I had no idea I was this hungry," she said around a mouthful of banana. She swallowed hard, disturbed by her own lack of manners. "I shouldn't be surprised, though. I haven't had anything to eat since last night."

"Well, there's plenty here." He stretched out one tanned arm and plucked another banana from the bunch. "But we should leave them on the tree until we're ready to eat. They'll stay fresher that way."

Amanda nodded and took the second banana from him. "So, how are we going to get out of here? Do you think any ships pass close enough to the island to see a signal fire?"

"I doubt it. Besides, we have more pressing problems on our hands." He peeled a banana for himself and took a third of it in one bite.

"Such as?"

"Water. If we don't find a source of drinking water, we won't live long enough to get rescued." He devoured the rest of the banana, tossing away the peel and reaching for another.

"Well, we're in the tropics, right? And it rains a lot in the tropics. All we have to do is collect rain water and we're set."

"Maybe. But collect it in what?" He gave her a moment to ponder this, and then continued. "If the island is large enough, there might be a spring-fed lake or stream. That's our best bet."

"Or maybe it's not really an island at all, but a peninsula."

"Might be," he said, thinking. "And in that case, all we have to do is walk to the nearest town."

Amanda peered into the banana bunch, checking for spiders, and then took another for herself. "I guess we should have a look around, then."

They moved off, he in the lead, Amanda padding carefully behind him. Her feet were still bare and, though she had spent most of her childhood tromping about Maine in her bare feet, pumps and deck shoes had softened her feet somewhat. The dried leaves felt like burlap to her and the stones cut like razors. She tried not to show her discomfort, but she knew he wasn't buying any of it.

"You know what I find strange? We haven't seen any animals around here . . . except for our friendly little spiders back there."

"You're right." She twisted up her face and thought for a moment, the pain in her feet forgotten for the moment. "Maybe this is one of those islands they tested the atomic bombs on and it's still uninhabitable."

He laughed at that and the sound echoed through the trees. "Atomic bomb! Where do you get this stuff?"

"I read an article once that explained all about the testing."

"I think you read too many of those science fiction books, that's what I think."

"Well, the article told the effects that the radiation had on the. . . ."

Amanda was stopped in her tracks as he shoved out his arm. Splayed fingers came to rest on her chest and she staggered backward a few steps. "Do you hear that?"

She listened. A dull roar issued from the thick brush ahead of them, slightly to the right. "It sounds like rushing water."

"Exactly." He cocked that boyish grin at her again and jerked a thumb to the right.

She followed. She was quite sure she was blushing, that her eyes were stinging not from the hot air, but from the shame of the entire situation.

Ahead of them, just on the other side of a large stand of bushes, was a waterfall. Greg stopped dead in his tracks and parted the brush, risking a glance over his shoulder at Amanda. "A waterfall. I think our problems are solved." He forged ahead, not waiting for her to follow, but holding the bushes apart as though she must.

It was beautiful in a way that Amanda had only imagined. The water, crystal clear and still foaming from its journey over the edge of the huge hill, pooled at the bottom and then ran off in an ever-smaller stream. She reached the edge of the water, stooped, and dipped one hand into it. Bringing that hand to her lips, she tasted it, smiling as she looked up at him. "No salt."

"Fabulous!" He stooped to test it for himself, and then smiled at her. "Problem number one solved. Now, if we can find ourselves some shelter, we're in business."

"If we can get rescued, we're in business. I don't know about you, but I have no desire to spend the rest of my life on this island."

She stood and walked away, enchanted by the waterfall, the seemingly untouched beauty of the scene. The water cascaded over the hill, fell in a solid sheet into the lake, then ran away. But there was something behind that sheet of water, something dark and deep and hidden from her.

She lifted her pants legs and tested the water with one foot, then settled both feet firmly on the sandy bottom of the small lake. The sand was wet and soft and it squished between her toes, threatening to suck her feet into it. Still, she stepped carefully, moving closer to the waterfall and whatever might be behind it.

"What are you doing?" When Amanda glanced back at him, he was smiling, his hands planted firmly on his hips. Clearly, he didn't intend to follow.

"There's something back here. I think it might be a cave." She pressed forward, stepping up on a little ledge and levering herself up to the small platform created by years of running water.

There was a good five feet of clearance between the falling water and the opening to the cave. Amanda stood on the cold, wet rocks and peered into utter darkness. She bit into her lip and frowned, wishing for some light.

"Be careful. You don't know what's in there."

She pondered this for a moment, ruling out such things as bears and mountain lions. There could be any number of nasty things in there, though, and she wasn't willing to risk being attacked. "We need some light. I can't see a thing. But I think it might be big enough to use as a shelter."

"Unless it's already occupied."

She jerked her head back and peeked around the rushing water. Just then, she was very afraid of what might be inside that cave. She climbed down from the ledge, somewhat more quickly than she had climbed up, and without the same concern for falling. If there were snakes in that cave, or bats or rats, she'd rather take a fall than face them.

"We can go back to the boat and get the flashlight. In fact, there's probably a lot of stuff in that boat we can use."

"Good deal. Let's do that, and then we can check out the cave." Just as she reached that last stretch of rock along the edge of the water, he held out his hand to help her ashore. "Can I ask just one stupid question?"

She took his hand readily and let her feet rest on dry land. "Sure."

"What in the world were you thinking, going out without any shoes?"

She looked down at her wet, wiggling toes and giggled. "Well, I figured no shoes were better than the satin slippers I was wearing. So, I tossed them before I got on the boat."

He nodded knowingly, cocked that smile of his again, and then moved off toward the boat. "How did you know where I was?"

"I heard your SOS on the radio. You said something about an island. There's only one island I know of that's close enough for your signal to have come from. So, I headed for it."

"And ended up here."

"Wherever here is." She nodded and sighed.

"I'm sorry I got you into this mess. I don't even really understand how you received my signal. It was only broadcast on a military channel."

"Must have been the weather. Anyway, it's my own stupid fault for being so rash. The first time in my entire life I ever took a risk and look what happened."

The boat lay ahead, cocked to one side and looking forlorn. Amanda stared at it for a moment, the memories of fishing trips and water skiing flooding her mind. She was very glad that her father wasn't there to see it.

"So, where'd you get this boat, anyway?" The sound of his voice broke her reverie, snapping her back to reality with a gasp.

"Actually, it's my father's boat. Was." One hand brushed back her hair, the other shielded her eyes from the sun.

"He's probably not going to be very happy when he finds out what happened to it."

"My father died three years ago."

"Oh, I'm sorry." He placed one hand on her shoulder, felt the awkwardness of it and pulled back. "Were you very close?"

"Mother died right after I was born, so it was always just Daddy and me. We did almost everything together. And the housekeeper kept things up so we still had time for fishing trips and such."

"He never remarried?"

Amanda shook her head. "No."

"Hey, maybe he had something going with the housekeeper, eh?" He elbowed her in the ribs and winked.

Her face flamed. Eyes narrowed and fists clenched, she spun on him, her gaze blistering his flesh. "My father mourned my mother every single day of his life. There was no room for any other woman in his heart, or in his . . . bed." She felt the hot sting of tears in her eyes and the desperate need to hit him. "How dare you suggest such a thing!"

She spun again and made for the boat in spliced steps that sent gales of sand flying up in their wake. Once she had reached the low side, she grabbed onto the rail and tried to hoist herself up. The boat creaked a bit, shifted. But in the end she wasn't strong enough to pull herself up over the edge.

"I'll give you a leg up."

She glared at him, still mad but knowing that she needed the help. She placed her hands on the rim of the deck and waited for the step of his cupped hands. Then she hoisted herself up over the edge and stood in the crook created by the meeting of deck and seat. "We can use these seat cushions for bedding. It'll be a lot more comfortable than the hard ground." She hefted two of them up to her shoulder then tossed them over the side, aiming for his head and watching with satisfaction as he dodged them. Then she grabbed the rest and added them to her arsenal.

Moving from one compartment to the next, she grabbed life vests and the first aid kit, the flashlights and flare gun. She threw them all at him, watching him dodge as he could and catch what he couldn't dodge. To his credit, he took it all without a word of complaint or retaliation. In the end, she decided to find it endearing and forgive him . . . eventually.

She leaped down from the boat, landing squarely in the sand and blowing back a lock of her hair. The two gathered armloads of gear and headed back into the brush, hoping to make it back to the cave and get settled before the sun slipped to the other side of the island.

"I'm really sorry about that comment," he said to her back as they trudged along. For a moment, the tone of his voice reminded her of Scott and goose bumps raced up her arms. "I didn't mean to insult your father. Really I didn't."

"I know." She shifted the load in her arms and walked a bit more slowly, letting him catch up. "It's just that Daddy and I were so close . . . I guess I just can't imagine there being any other woman in his life. Nobody but Mother and me, I mean."

"I understand." He drew up next to her, matching her pace. He didn't look directly at her, but she could feel his gaze shift every now and again. "It's good that you two had each other."

She chuckled a bit at that, finally gracing him with a little smile. "My girlfriend, Dana, says that my father is responsible for my inability to have a long-term relationship."

"Oh really?" He returned her smile, making her look away for a moment. The sudden closeness made her heart speed, her head spin. "And is your friend Dana a psychiatrist?"

"Oh no! She's just a well-meaning friend who reads way too many women's magazines. But she says that my mother's death and the death of my fiancé, coupled with the close relationship I had with my deceased father gives me separation issues and a fear of intimacy."

"I don't suppose she offered any cure?" His eyes sparkled at that. She couldn't decide whether he was poking fun of Dana or at her, but she decided not to spoil the mood.

"She says I push people away out of the fear they will leave me if I fall in love with them."

"So, what you need, then, is someone to prove to you that not everyone you love will leave?"

There was a moment of silence. It hung heavily around them and made Amanda's throat tighten. "That's just what she says." A frown darkened her face for a moment and she turned away. "And . . . that's probably way more information than you needed to know."

"If it's any consolation, I have zero luck at relationships, too."

"Really?" Her face brightened and for the first time, she noticed that he had dimples.

"My father and I fought like cats and dogs. My mother died when I was ten. I didn't date much in high school, but right after I graduated, I fell in love with the most amazing woman. Her name was Wanda and she had hair like sunshine. Anyway, when I was drafted, she promised she'd write every day. She said she'd wait for me and when the war was over and I came home, we'd be married."

"Aw, that's so sweet! You're lucky to have found someone who loves you that much."

"Oh yes! Sweet. Except for the fact that two weeks after I shipped out, she married my best friend, Eddie."

"I'm so sorry." She hung her head for a moment in pity and when she looked up, the waterfall was directly in front of her.

"Yea, me too." He dropped his load to the ground and fished the flashlight out of his back pocket. "Everything happens for a purpose though, right?"

She nodded.

"Then, maybe it was for the best. Maybe, us being here has a higher purpose, too."

Amanda's mind raced and she found that her palms had begun to sweat. Just then, he was looking at her the way a man might look at the turkey just before he carved it. She let the seat cushions fall from her arms and she turned away, caught between embarrassment and wishful thinking.

"Maybe it does," she muttered.

When she turned back to him, he was flicking the flashlight on and off, testing the switch and watching the beam of light. "I'll go check out our new home away from home. Just in case there's some awful beast in there, I have my trusty dusty Swiss army knife to protect me." He patted his front left pocket and smiled.

"Be careful. There might be bears." She followed him to the edge of the water, peering between rock and water to watch his progress. For one brief moment, her heart stopped as she wondered what would happen to her if he were killed or injured. Then she pushed the thought from her mind and called out to him. "Everything okay in there?"

"Everything's great," he hollered back, sticking his head out of the cave and smiling. "Come on up!"

Cautiously, she made her way up the stones to the small rock platform that marked their new home. Greg stood in the middle of the cave, the flashlight playing over the walls and floor. Small stalactites hung from the ceiling and several niches had been created in the walls by running water. Still, there didn't seem anything menacing in the dark recesses of the cave.

"It's certainly big enough. And it seems dry. From the look of things, I don't think we'll have to share." He let the light play slowly over the ceiling. "Not even with bats."

"Bats?" She instinctively ducked and covered her head. She hadn't thought of such a thing, but now that the thought had entered her mind, she found it terrifying. Feet shuffling along the ground, she edged closer to him. "There aren't any bats in here. Are there?"

"Not at the moment. And if there were bats, they'd certainly be in here during the daylight hours."

She relaxed a bit, letting her shoulders loosen and exhaling audibly. "Well, that's good to know. Bats are . . . icky."

"No bats. I promise. So, shall we move in now?"

Rubbing her sweaty palms briskly on her pants, she smiled and nodded. "Let's."

They made several trips back to the shore, collecting their gear and stowing it in the back of the cave. Amanda set about laying out the seat cushions and life vests, one makeshift bed on each side of the cave. It wasn't like they had any clothes to change into or would need any privacy. She just didn't want him to think she was a scared little girl or—God forbid!—forward.

"I'm going to go collect some more food," he said, clapping his hands together once and smiling. "I don't know about you, but I'm getting hungry again."

"It's a pity those coconuts are so far up in the trees. We need to figure out a way to get them down."

"I'll work on that tomorrow. In the meantime, why don't you see if you can scout out a good place for . . . ?" He paused for a moment, trying to find a more delicate way of putting what he had nearly blurted out. "Private business."

She stared at him blankly, confused. Then it snapped into place. "Oh! Yes. Okay."

The idea hadn't occurred to her before, but now that it had been presented to her, she found the need almost overwhelming. Without another word, she followed him down the rocks to the shore, parting ways with him at that point and venturing off into the jungle.

When she returned to the cave, Greg was seated at the center, a large rock in one hand and a coconut in the other. He looked up as she entered and smiled. "Look what I found!" He shook the coconut in the air, his eyes catching a ray of light.

"How did you manage that?"

"I found it lying on the ground. I don't know if it's any good, but I figured it was worth a shot. Doesn't look like it's been off the tree very long."

"Well, good luck getting it open." She moved to sit on the ground across from him, anxious to watch the proceedings. "Oh, and as for that other thing . . . head to your right and it's by the large rock in the stand of Hibiscus bushes."

He nodded solemnly and removed the knife from his pocket, selecting the Phillips head screwdriver and placing it over one of the eyes in the coconut. A swift blow with the rock and a hole was punched in the shell. Another blow and the shell was ventilated. He handed the coconut over to her with a grin.

As she reached out, her fingers grazed his, sending a shiver up her arm and straight to her core. She nearly pulled back, but then thought better of it. He was handsome, that was true. But there was more to him, much more. It made her heart trip over itself and her head swim. And if a simple brush of flesh against flesh could cause such a reaction, what might happen if she actually found herself in his arms?

CHAPTER THREE

Sunlight stole into the cave between rock and water, slashing across Amanda's face as she slept. She felt the warmth of it and rolled over, trying to find a patch of shadow in which to open her eyes. Lashes fluttered and she yawned, arms stretching out wide as she slid into consciousness.

She sat up, momentarily lost and confused in the new surroundings. It all came back to her slowly, as the sound of rushing water filled her ears. One glance to the right told her that she was alone. Once her eyes had focused, she spied the coconut shell from the previous night. Only now, it was filled with water and held a bright purple orchid. Next to it stood a note, hastily scrawled on the back of another note, written long ago and typed on thin paper. It was an old note from Greg's traitorous fiancé. Amanda read the back before turning to the note intended for her:

Amanda:
Hope you slept well. Sorry I had to leave you.
Greg

She put down the note quickly, as though it might bite her. Her hand was shaking and she could feel a lump at the back of her throat. He had left her. Somehow, some way, he had gone and left her to fend for herself.

Like a rocket, she was up off the makeshift bed and racing toward the mouth of the cave. Greg was nowhere to be seen, either in the water or on the shore. As quickly as was safely possible, she made her way down the rocks to the sand below. Then she called for him.

No answer.

The bushes tore at her as she dashed through the jungle, mindless of what she was stepping on or what might lash out at her. She halfway expected to reach the beach and find the boat gone, though she knew it wasn't possible. The hole in the side had been large and there was certainly nothing on the island with which to repair it. But maybe another boat had come along. Maybe Greg had allowed himself to be rescued without even going back for her.

The bushes rustled, fighting against her for a moment and then spitting her out onto the dry sand. Before her lay the water, the bluest horizon she had ever seen, and Greg.

Her breath came in huge gulps, her head swimming as she bent to catch her breath, hands pressed to her knees and fighting not to topple over. If Greg had heard her stumbling through the bushes, he paid her no heed. He was bare chested, feet resting on the sand and his pants rolled up to the knees. Still, the bottom of those pants was wet. He held a long tree branch in his hands and at the end of it dangled a length of fishing line. He was fishing and his expression was near rapturous.

"Having any luck?" she called, smiling and trying to act casual.

He turned to look at her, his face lighting up. "Well, good morning, sleepy head. I'm afraid the fish just aren't cooperating today."

She made her way across the squishy sand to stand next to him. "Where'd you get the fishing line?"

"Oh, I came down here to take another crack at that radio. I'm afraid you're right. The battery must be dead. But I found some fishing line in one of the compartments."

She nodded. "I think salt water must have gotten to the battery. And did you find hooks in there, too?"

"No, actually. I found one in the sand. Stepped right on it, which is how the whole thing began."

"Ooh, that must have hurt something awful!" She made a face and shook her head. "Would you like me to take a look at it for you? Can't be too careful."

"It was the straight end, not the barbed end. Nothing terrible."

"But Tetanus . . ."

He leaned over comically and whispered in her ear. "It's fine. Really. Stop worrying, Mom."

For his efforts, she rewarded him with a dirty look. "Whatever you say. So, what are you using for bait?"

"There are these little schools of fishes that swim right up to the shore line. I just bent over the water and waited for them to swim close enough, then I scooped them up on shore."

"How ingenious of you. And, I do wish you luck." She paused for a moment, watching the water and the clouds, somehow more at peace than she had been in over a year. "Thank you for the flower, by the way. It was a lovely gesture."

"My pleasure."

"Next time, you might reconsider the wording of your note. I got the impression that you had somehow found a way off the island and had left me here to rot."

Greg's head whipped around and his smile faltered. "I'm such a dolt! Why do I keep sticking my foot in it?" He nearly lost the fishing pole in an effort to smack himself on the forehead. "What I meant to say is that I was sorry I had to just leave a note instead of being there when you woke up."

"You gave me quite a start. But it's all better now." Suddenly, she discovered that her hand was resting on his arm. She stared at it in disbelief, as though it belonged to someone else. Presently, she noticed that he was staring at it, too. Her face blazed with color and she struggled to find a graceful way out. In the end, there was nothing she could do but slide her hand off his arm and hope he didn't read too much into it.

"I'm going to scout out some more food sources. And I want to climb to the top of our little mountain and take a look at the rest of the island. We don't know. There could be a beach resort on the other side of the island. Good luck with the fishing."

And with that, she turned and ran across the beach, into the bushes.

The mountain which gifted them with the waterfall was not tall, but as far as Amanda could see, it was the highest point on the island. She imagined that, from the top of it, she could see most of the island and possibly any other islands which lie beyond. The problem was how to get to the top.

From her vantage point, climbing that mountain was a Herculean task. There was a rise to the ground, a gentle slope which would take her at least a third of the way. After that, it was grab and pull, boost and hoist. She stared at the top, squinting against the bright sky and wondering.

"One foot in front of the other," she said to the mountain and no one else in particular.

She walked part of the way, feeling the slope of the land pull at her calves and the heat of the day soak into her skin. This was unequivocally the most beautiful place on the face of the earth. But everything here was such a chore.

She had kept walking, letting her mind wander, taking a moment now and again to pause and admire a giant flower. Everything grew well here, clearly besting their domestic counterparts by leaps and bounds.

And before she knew it, she had reached that point where she could no longer walk, but would have to climb. It's not that she was weak or lazy. She was quite strong for her size. But she wasn't exactly athletic, now was she? Most of her life had been spent in a chair, behind a desk.

The rocks were blissfully shaded and cool to her touch as she grabbed them, pushing with feet and pulling with hands. The slope here wasn't as steep as it might have been and for that she was thankful. Some hundred yards further found her red-faced and struggling, the perspiration tracing streaks of dust and dirt down her face. Through concentration, she found her rhythm, that particular symphony of motion that made her arms and legs work in concert, propelling her upward in a slow but steady dance.

Some sort of euphoria overcame her and she began to smile. Conquering this little mountain was possibly the toughest task she had set for herself in all her life. And just as she was thanking the mountain for this opportunity, she found that she had reached the top.

The peak of the mountain was small but what there was of it was flat. A large boulder sat at the back of it and as Amanda stood, the horizon rose to meet her gaze. She placed one hand on the boulder, steadying herself as a great suck of air filled her lungs.

She could see the whole of the island from where she stood. Even crouched as she was, the great ocean stretched out before her. To one side, Greg stood on the beach, the makeshift pole still in his hand. He was little more than a child's toy from where she stood. Completely to the other side, a large expanse of the island stretched out its hand, for it was indeed hand-shaped. It was as though some giant had fallen, his outstretched hand reaching for the ocean. Its fingertips created a lagoon of sorts, a calm little cove where birds might play and the dolphins might swim. The thought made her smile and for a moment, she nearly forgot that she was standing at the top of a very small mountain.

Sadly, she could locate no sign of human life anywhere. There was no hoped-for resort nor even a tent or lean-to. But there were fruit trees and palm trees aplenty. They might not get help, but they wouldn't starve.

"Greg!" she called as loud as she could. He failed to turn around, so she tried for more volume. "Greg!"

He turned then and she waved madly, hoping he would spot her. After several seconds of a mad search, he spotted her waving form and waved back. "What do you see?"

"Nothing at all," she screamed.

The exchange ended there and she found herself faced with the task of climbing back down the mountain. One would think that the climbing-down would be much easier than the climbing-up but Amanda found this not to be true. Her muscles already ached and there was no goal left to her as there had been when she climbed up.

Hand over hand and foot against rock, she made her way slowly toward the ground. At one point, the rock she had clutched in her right hand broke loose, dropping her a yard or so before she managed to catch herself with her foot. She hung there, motionless, as she tried to quiet her nerves and catch her breath. She continued then, rejoicing when her feet finally struck the ground.

The air was hot and so humid that one could nearly drown just from the breathing of it. Her clothes clung to her skin and her hair was matted to her forehead. She'd have traded her last bite of food for a nice hot shower.

For the moment, there was only the slightly cooler water of the pond and the scent of whatever flower she could find. If nothing else, the water would take away some of the heat that seemed to permeate her flesh. Greg would be on the beach for a while, she guessed, at least long enough for her to take a quick dip.

With a last testing glance over her shoulder, she worked at the buttons on her blouse. She let it slip from her shoulders, drizzle down her fingertips and puddle at her feet. Then she removed her jeans. She wanted everything clean, but she didn't want herself weighed down by the wet clothing.

With one foot, she tested the safety of the pond's floor. It seemed solid enough and didn't have a steep slope. So, she slipped into the water, testing her footing with each step and dragging her clothes after her. Where the water of the ocean had been warm, this water was a good twenty degrees cooler. It felt amazing against her skin as it rushed past. She lowered herself carefully, bending backward a bit and letting her hair sink into the water. Then she set to washing her clothes.

Once she had cleaned the clothes as best she could with just water, she tossed them up onto the shore so she could swim a bit. She had no idea how deep that pond might be, but being able to swim in such clear, perfectly cool water was a delight. It rushed past gently, instead of crashing by in waves. It brushed over her skin instead of beating at it.

"This is like a fairy tale come true," she said to no one in particular, and headed off toward the falls.

Time slipped away as she swam and she found herself smiling without cause. In all her life, she could not remember another time when she had felt as free and happy as she did right at that moment.

"Wow! That looks like a lot more fun than fishing!"

Amanda screamed and spun in search of the voice. There stood Greg, pole and fish in hand, smiling for all he was worth. She dove under the water, managing to conceal everything but her crimson face and neck.

"How long have you been standing there?" If anything, her voice was threatening.

"About ten seconds is all."

"You . . . you turn around. And don't peek." She was shaking hard and her voice would scarcely rise above a squeak. "And don't turn back until I tell you."

Ever the gentleman, Greg turned around, though she was quite sure he was grinning in amusement. She waded toward the shore, stretching to snatch up her clothes. By now, they were only a tad less wet and their time on the beach had coated them with enough sand to make a second rinse necessary.

"You stay turned around, now. Don't you dare peek!"

She swished the clothes around in the water and slipped into her shirt, buttoning only two buttons before trying to struggle into her jeans. They proved quite the problem, all tight and clinging to her skin.

"These fish will go bad if you take too long."

Her voice was shrill and panicked. "Don't you dare turn around!"

She fought harder against the relentless grip of wet denim, finally managing to get the jeans over her hips, though the button resisted her efforts. In desperation, she climbed part way out of the water and jerked both halves together, wrestling the button securely into its hole, then fumbling with the buttons on her blouse once more.

"Okay. You can turn around now." She was still flushed and panting. Her heart still beat against her ribcage.

"All better now?"

She tossed back a lock of hair in a huff and nodded. "All better."

"Good. I caught the fish. You clean them." He thrust out the stringer of dead fish and smiled.

Amanda glanced at the fish, and then looked back at Greg, cocking one hip to the side and folding her arms over her chest. "You think because I'm a girl I can't clean a fish? Fine! Give them here!" She held out one hand.

Greg smiled and placed the stringer in her hand. "Have fun." Instantly, he laid down the pole and began unfastening his uniform pants.

"What do you think you're doing?" Her eyes were wide, her mouth agape.

"You know, for a nice lady, you sure do yell a lot." There was that smile again, all broad and full of warmth. "I'm going for a swim."

"Well, you could wait until I'm gone before you go getting all . . . all . . . naked."

"Then go."

"I will."

"Fine."

"Fine!"

She spun on one heel and marched away, the fish dancing at the end of the string. She had gone no more than fifty feet when she realized that she had nothing with which to clean the fish. The only knife—or tool, for that matter—that they had was still in Greg's possession. Ruefully, she turned back and hurried to the clearing.

"If I'm going to clean the fish, I'll need your knife," she announced loudly as she burst from the bushes.

He was already in the water, his pants lying in a disheveled heap on the sand. "I was wondering when you'd realize that. Here, I'll get it." He began marching toward her, the water receding over his belly as he drew closer.

"No!" she yelled, thrusting out both hands and waving them frantically. "I'll get it."

That smile lit his face again, all sunshine and sex, protection and promises. "Oh, I'm not the least bit modest. Besides, I know right where it is."

"I'll find it. Honestly!" She stooped at once, her back toward him . . . just in case. She rummaged through his pants hurriedly, finally laying hands on the knife. "Got it. See ya!"

Knife firmly in hand, she raced back into the bushes to where the fish lay waiting.

She had gone fishing with her father so often that things like baiting hooks and cleaning fish were second nature to her. Once she had secured a flat enough rock on which to work, the task went very quickly. She gathered the fish filets into a large leaf, pocketed the knife and headed back to the pond. Whistling as she approached, just to warn Greg, she finally stepped out of the bushes.

"All done." Both man and pants were gone and Amanda wrinkled her brow as she headed for the cave.

It was somewhat harder, making her way up the stones with an armload of fish. She was not by nature a graceful lady, and the slippery rocks made the task all the harder. When she finally gained the entrance to the cave, darkness swallowed her and she could see little more than shadow on shadow. If Greg were inside, he made no noise.

"Greg?" She listened to the silence. "Are you here?"

"On the bed," was his soft reply. "I didn't want to waste flashlight time. Pity we can't find a permanent way to get some light in here."

"Perhaps if we had a mirror or something." She felt her way to the small outcropping of rocks at the center of the cave and stooped to lay the fish on it. "The fish are all cleaned. We should cook them as soon as possible."

"We can't risk a fire in here. I'll go down and collect some firewood. I suppose at this point, making a permanent fire pit isn't out of the question."

She nodded as though he could see her, and then felt the breeze as he passed, so close that she could almost feel the fabric of his pants. Another shudder took her, making her sit down hard on the ground.

"After we eat, we should start a signal fire. Or maybe spell out the word 'help' on the beach. Anything to help our chances."

When no answer was forthcoming, she turned around to find that he'd already gone. For long moments she sat there, suddenly wondering if they would ever get off the island at all. The past two days had been a lark, an adventure. But she couldn't continue that way. She needed a hot shower and a real bed. She needed to get back to her life before she lost her job and her father's house.

Her house. Her father was gone. Scott was gone. And no matter how she fought it, she couldn't get them back.

"How's about bringing those fish? Or are you into sushi?"

Amanda shook her head and stood up quickly, barking her shin on the rock as she bent to gather the fish. It throbbed all the way down, pulsed as she walked. By the time she reached Greg and the fire, she was limping.

"You okay? What happened?"

She looked down at her leg, mildly scuffed and only pink from the abrasion. Already it was starting to turn purple. It made her feel stupid and clumsy . . . again.

"I just banged my leg on a rock. It'll be fine."

"You sit. I'll cook the fish." He took the leaf bundle from her and unwrapped it. "But tomorrow night, it's your turn."

"Deal." She sat down as gracefully as was possible and began rubbing her leg.

"You know, the swelling might go down quicker if you put your leg in the water."

"I told you, I'll be fine." Already, the edges of her cheeks had begun to grow hot.

He nodded and placed the bundled fish on a small piece of metal grating he had found, and then leaned back against the tree. "So, have you always lived in Maine?"

"All my life . . . same town . . . same house." She looked at him briefly and smiled. "How about you?"

"Fairbury, Nebraska. I was born and raised on the same farm. I was actually relieved to get drafted. It got me the hell out of there."

"Still, don't you miss your family?"

He shrugged. It was exaggerated and forced. "I guess. And I'll probably end up going back there eventually. I have this friend back at the base. His name is Bob Stevens. We used to pull guard duty all the time and we'd talk for hours, make plans for when we got out. We're going to open up our own garage. Maybe back in Fairbury. Maybe someplace totally new."

Amanda's head snapped around, her eyes burned. "Bob Stevens? That's my grandfather's name. Was." Goose bumps raced up and down her arms.

"Hmmm . . . quite a coincidence. Not a rare name, though." He leaned forward and peeled back a portion of the leaf, checking the fish, and then covering it again.

"I suppose not. So, were you good in school? Did you like it?"

"I hated school. The only reason I went is to get out of the farm chores. You?"

"Loved it. I was on the honor roll every year. Joined the chess club, the glee club. Went on to college."

"Oh, an egghead, huh?" He proffered a slight grin and leaned back against the tree again. "First love?"

She blushed. It was so instant and so intense that she couldn't have hidden it for the world. "Scott. My fiancé. Well, if you don't count that guy on Star Trek."

"Star Trek? What's that?"

She made an exaggerated jaw-dropping motion and gasped. "You have to be kidding me! Only the biggest cult TV show in the history of the world. Don't you ever watch TV?"

"Amanda, I have no clue what you're talking about. I've read books. Listened to the radio. But I have no clue what TV is. I told you, I've been out of the country for a long time."

"You know, TV? Pictures and sound coming through little wires into this box?"

"Oh, movies, right?"

"No. Not in a theater. In your house. Television." As she stared at him, he shook his head. "What are you, Amish?"

"Methodist, actually."

She nodded, the motion of it dropping a strand of hair over one eye. She brushed it back hurriedly and smiled. "Catholic here."

Greg poked the fire with a thin stick and sniffed the air. "So, how did your Scott die?"

"A car accident. A drunk driver fell asleep at the wheel. His car jumped the median and hit Scott's car." She paused for a moment, biting viciously into her lip to stave off the tears. "He lived for several days but, in the end, there wasn't much they could do for him.

"I'm so sorry. It must have been so hard on you, losing him so suddenly."

She nodded slowly, her eyes swelling from the potential tears. For a few moments, she couldn't speak as she tried to gain control of herself. Then, she cleared her throat and changed the subject. "Well, if you don't watch TV, what do you do for fun?"

"I read. Listen to the radio. Occasionally I go to the movies. But mostly I like to go to baseball games when I can."

She watched him remove the fish from the fire. He placed it on another rock, still steaming, and peeled back the leaf to let the steam out. The smell reached her nostrils and her stomach growled. In all her life, she had never smelled anything so divine.

"Dig in," he said with a wave of his hand.

"A baseball fan, eh? What's your team?"

"I've always had a passion for the Cubs. But out in the boonies where we lived, best we could do were a few college teams."

"For me, it was video games," she said around a mouthful of fish. The taste was so sweet she nearly swooned.

"I'm afraid I don't know what video games are, either."

"Wow! Fairbury must be one very backward place." She checked his face, making sure she hadn't offended him.

"That it is." He chuckled a bit and tilted his head to look at her. "You know, when you smile like that, you look just like Elizabeth Taylor. Well, if she was a brunette, I mean."

"Really?" Oddly, she found the thought appealing. "Nobody's ever told me that before."

"Maybe nobody's ever really looked at you."

She looked down then, realizing that the fish was nearly gone. Her stomach was nearly full as well, so she leaned back against her tree and sighed in complete contentment. "Ready to go build that signal fire?"

"I've been thinking about that. Setting a signal fire might work against us, actually. I mean, what if the wrong people saw it?"

Amanda scrunched up her brow and frowned at him. "The wrong people? What are you talking about? I'll tell you, right at this moment, I don't care if we're rescued by drug dealers or pirates or what. I just want to get out of here."

"No. You know. The Japanese. If they showed up instead of an Allied ship or plane, we could be captured."

"Captured? Who the hell would capture us?" She sat forward suddenly, alarmed.

"The Japanese, of course. They have control of most of these islands these days."

"Hold the phone, Greg! The Japanese have been our friends since right after the end of World War II. Did you hit your head in that plane crash or what?"

Greg was off his feet, shoving off from the palm tree and staring her down as she struggled to stand. "I think you're the one who hit her head. We only just got involved in this war. And unless I missed a bulletin two days ago, we haven't yet won it."

She pressed both hands to her head and shook it, hobbling slowly about with wide eyes. "No, no, no! See, this is 2012 and World War Two ended over sixty years ago."

"Okay, now I know you're crazy! We only just got into this war when the Japs bombed Pearl Harbor. Nobody's won it. We just got here."

"Wait! What year were you born?" She stood stock still, waiting for his answer.

"Nineteen twenty-two."

"No way!" She shook her finger at him and sneered.

"I can prove it." He reached into his back pocket and pulled out his wallet. After a few seconds of flipping through things, he pulled out a card and shoved it at her.

Amanda studied his face, searching for signs of faulty deception, and then took the card. It was his Nebraska state driver's license, due to expire in three months. On it was his birthday: October 28, 1922. Amanda began to shake.

CHAPTER FOUR

"This isn't possible. It's not." She passed the license back with one trembling hand, felt the sting of terrified tears at the corners of her eyes. "I left Maine two days ago, on May 14, 2012."

"And you ended up in the South Pacific in 1943." Greg sat down hard, his face growing paler by the second. "It can't happen."

"It can't." She joined him on the ground. "I couldn't receive your signal across thousands of miles and sixty years."

Silence pressed in, hard and fast. Amanda could fight it no more and tears traced dusty lines down her cheeks. To her right, Greg pulled the dog tags from under his half-open shirt and looked at them. "Twenty-two." He slipped them back inside his shirt and folded his arms around his knees.

She cocked her head and peered at him, her lip trembling. She swallowed hard and when she spoke, her voice was little more than a whisper. "When I was on the boat, heading for your position, there was this light . . . thing."

His head jerked up, eyes flashing and more color draining from his face. "I saw it. But I thought it was the Aurora Borealis . . . or something like it."

"It swept right over the boat. When it did, it slowed things down. So much so that it nearly swept me off the stern of the boat."

"It was off in the distance. It didn't touch me." He stared at his boots for a moment, his brow furrowed and his lips pressed tightly together. "What do you suppose it was?"

"I have no idea. But I know I'm really scared right now." She wanted him to hold her. No matter that it was improper; she wanted him to hold her more than anything. "Because if we really are in 1943, then I may never get back to my own time. Not that I really have anything to go back to."

Her body shook hard as she began to cry again, her sobs coming faster and more furious. She pressed her hands to her face, still shaking. Suddenly, there was an arm around her, then two. When she pulled her hands away, Greg had scooted next to her and had her in a tight grasp. Without a thought, she dropped her head to his chest and let him stroke her hair. All things considered, it was the safest she'd felt since she was a little girl.

One hand slid up her arm to her head, pressing it tighter against his chest, and then stroking her hair. "Ssh," he cooed. "It's going to be all right."

Amanda jerked her head up and craned her neck to look at him. "How, Greg? How is it going to be all right?"

Whether to console her further, or to prevent her from seeing the fear in his eyes, he pressed her face back to his chest again. "I don't know. But it will." He began rocking then, a slow and steady motion that Amanda found more dizzying than comforting. "I promise."

She had no idea how long she let him hold her, but when she finally shifted and began to pull away, his shirt was soaked with tears. There was no doubt that she looked quite the sight, face red and streaked with tears, eyes puffy. She swiped at her nose with the back of her hand and coughed. One hand ran through her hair and she sat upright again.

"We'll figure this out. We have to. I can't stay here. This isn't my time or place."

Greg nodded and sat up a little straighter. If he was scared, his face betrayed none of it. "We know what year we're in. We know our approximate position. And we're pretty sure what caused it."

"We just don't have a name for it." She nodded briefly and rested her head against the tree trunk, eyes locked on the dim sky. "If we knew what the hell that thing was . . ."

"But we don't. We might never know. And we don't know if it will come back again."

"And if it does, whether I can go back through it and get home safely. For all we know, I have to hit the thing in exactly the same boat at exactly the same spot in the ocean." She sighed and hugged herself tighter.

"The only thing we can do is try. And even if it doesn't work, would it really be so awful to be stuck in 1943?" He tried a smile on for size, but it just didn't fit quite right.

She looked at him, mind and heart battling fiercely. Part of her wanted to be home, safely in bed, right at that very moment. Part of her wanted to stay with Greg, no matter what, and see where it led. There was something about him that made her want to love him. "It wouldn't be awful," she offered. "Just terribly inconvenient."

"Look at it this way. You'll get the chance to meet your father again. As a young man."

She bit into her lip and fought back more tears. "Okay, now you're getting into conundrums and time travel and a whole lot of things I just don't want to be responsible for."

"Such as?"

"If I'm not supposed to be born until 1988, and I'm here, will I still be born in 1988? And if I meet my father and my mother, knowing that she will die in child birth, should I try to stop it? Can I stop it? Can I save Scott?" She leaped up from her spot beneath the tree and clamped both hands tightly on either side of her head. "I can't think about all this. I have to get home. I just have to."

Greg was at her back, one comforting hand on her arm, gripping it securely. It would have been so easy to just spin and fall into his arms just then. It would have even felt right. But Amanda couldn't let herself give in to it. It was more dangerous than being captured by the Japanese. If she fell in love with Greg, she wouldn't want to go home. Everything could change, and she wasn't sure she wanted to be responsible for that.

"We'll get you home. Don't worry. And the first step to doing that is to get off this island."

"Or find that . . . thing. And get out in the ocean somehow so I can go back through it." She nodded and drew in a deep breath. "We'll be able to see it at night, I think. I wish I had some binoculars."

"Too bad I'm not a diver instead of a pilot. There were binoculars on the plane."

She offered him a conciliatory smile and nodded. "What are the odds of somebody finding us here? I mean, don't you have some sort of homing beacon or tracking device in your plane? I thought all planes had them."

"No tracking device. This is 1943, remember?"

"Ah, yes. Well, maybe somebody heard your SOS?"

"I doubt it. There'd have been planes searching for me."

"That's another thing. If we're in the middle of the biggest war the world has ever seen, why haven't we heard any bombs or seen any ships or planes? How far are we from the action?"

He thrust his hands in his pockets and looked at the ground for a moment. "Since I don't know our exact position, I can't say. But it's not like there's a huge battle going on every minute of every day."

"True . . . I guess. But what if there is a battle? And what if they come here?"

"Is there anything else you'd like to worry about?" That boyish grin was reprised and his eyes twinkled with captured light. "Because if there's not, I'd like to go exploring a bit more. Maybe we can find some discarded tools or even a wild pig to eat."

"Okay, okay! So I worry too much. But just try and tell me I don't have a reason."

"Oh, you have reason all right. Now, would you care to join me? Or would you rather stay here and fend off the marauding Japanese all by yourself?" He held out his hand and she took it as though she had done so a million times before.

He was strong and confident and all the things she was not. She walked with him, his shadow covering her completely, and suddenly she wasn't afraid anymore.

There was nothing much to be seen in the rest of the jungle. The lack of birdsong and wildlife was still disturbing, but somehow she had even grown accustomed to the silence. The city was noisy and even her small home town boomed with the noise of animals, cars and radios. The quiet there was different, but peaceful.

Suddenly, Amanda stopped in her tracks, hauling up on Greg's arm and making him stagger backward momentarily. "Look here! I know what these are." She grabbed one of the tiny orange fruits and yanked it off the tree. "Daddy and I used to eat these all the time when we went to Florida to visit my aunt. They're cumquats."

Greg watched her carefully as she peeled back the skin and took a bite. He watched her face, the bliss as she chewed and swallowed. He followed suit, peeling the small fruit and popping it into his mouth whole. Then he pulled a face and nearly spat it out. "These are awful! They're bitter!"

"Well, yea. They're bitter, sure. But they're citrus and they'll keep us from getting scurvy and rickets and stuff."

"I'll risk it," he said and tossed the skins violently into the brush.

Amanda shrugged and began filling her pockets with the small fruit. Satisfied, she held out her own hand to him before she even realized she'd done it. He took it, his fingers sliding in to lace with hers, arm bulging a bit, drawing her nearer.

"So, is the future wonderful? What's it like?"

She laughed and tossed back her hair, the hint of a frown darkening her features as she realized what a girlish and flirtatious gesture it had been. "Well, we still have wars. But we have some pretty awesome stuff. Like the cars. They're not as nice as the cool old cars of the fifties, but they have stereos and air conditioning."

"In the cars? Hmm . . ."

"And hundreds of channels on the television. You'll like that because you can watch any team play any game, most any time you want. And if you can't watch it when it's on, you can record it on the DVR and watch it later."

"So, I could watch the Cubs? From my very own living room?"

"Yes, and if you have a really cool TV, you can watch the Dodgers in the picture-in-picture."

"Oh, I'm really going to like the future, I think."

She stopped dead in her tracks and dropped his hand, face caught somewhere between shock and joy. "Oh my God! I just realized something."

"What's that?" He watched her now, his gaze catching hers and not letting go.

"I know every movie that will be a success. Every TV show, every book that will be written. I even know who's going to win the World Series and Kentucky Derby in some cases. In fact, in about thirty years, I can invest a few dollars in Microsoft and we could be rich by the time the Internet comes around."

"What's the Internet?" He cocked his head to one side like a curious puppy and smiled.

"Well, it's kind of hard to explain. But almost every home in America has a computer. And almost all businesses in the world have a computer. So somebody came up with this method of connecting all the computers in the world through the telephone lines and bang! The internet was born."

He thought for a moment, his mouth screwed into an odd shape and his brow furrowed. "But what's it good for?"

Amanda's jaw dropped and she let loose a little chuckle. "Lots of things. You can chat with people from around the world. You get news and weather . . . even baseball scores. You can buy and sell and send electronic mail. I don't think people in the twenty-first century could survive without it."

"I guess I'll just have to wait until I get there to see what all the excitement's about." He held out his hand for hers this time. She took it readily.

"You'll like it. Trust me." They walked in silence for a few moments, her eyes on the ground and her face shadowed. "I wonder if it's ethical, though. Knowing what's going to happen before it happens?"

"Perhaps not. But would it really alter the course of the universe if you made a few bucks off of it?" There was that smile again, all sunshine and candy, telling her it would be all right.

"I suppose not." She gave his hand an involuntary little squeeze, and then blushed at the familiarity of it.

"I can make one prediction about the future, though."

"And what's that?"

He leaned in close, whispering into her ear. "If we don't get moving, we'll never get back to the cave before nightfall." His breath washed over her cheek, drawing a blush, tracing a shiver up her spine.

"Right." She moved off quickly, before he could see the blush.

"Just more beach," Greg sighed, placing his hands on his hips and frowning at the waves.

Amanda drew up beside him, brushing bits of spider webs off her arms as she stared at the vacant sand. "No Japanese encampments. No Honolulu Hilton."

"As much noise as we made crashing through the brush like that, if there had been any Japanese here, they'd have certainly heard us coming." His tone was snippy and sharp.

"Well, forgive me for not being experienced in jungle warfare. I'm more the Macy's bargain basement warrior myself."

"I'll pretend I know what that means." The long hike had made them both irritable and just now, his smile looked more like a pout.

After a few moments of staring at the horizon, she turned toward him and tried a smile. "I'm sorry. I'm just tired is all. And stressed."

"And a little smelly." He looked up suddenly, his face stricken. "Oh no! I meant me. Not you. You don't stink. You're. . . ."

She held up both hands, shaking her head and waving them. "It's all right. I do too. I know."

He looked frantically about, eyes searching the terrain for something. Then he darted off, the upper half of his body disappearing into a bush. When he returned, he held out one hand, smiling as he proffered a large red flower.

"You're nothing if not sweet," she giggled as she took the flower and tucked it behind one ear. Suddenly, her gaze shifted to some point behind him and her eyes widened. "Look! Aren't those pineapples?"

Greg spun, his eyes searching for phantom pineapples. "Why, they sure are!"

"Terrific! Because the fish has worn off and I'm starving."

"We'll cut a few and leave the others to ripen. Besides, I don't think we can carry them all home at once."

"Home?" Her expression was at once humorous and tender.

"Well, what passes for home for us, as long as we're here."

She nodded and walked with him to the small grove of pineapples. Using his knife, Greg managed to cut three of them free. Then, he filleted one of the fruits for their supper.

She took one of the chunks from him with a smile and bit off a large portion of it. Her face lit up and she moaned, smacking her lips for good measure. "I don't remember any canned pineapple tasting this sweet." She stuffed the last of it in her mouth and held out her hand for more.

"I've been on C-rations for too long. I couldn't tell you what pineapple tastes like. But this sure is good." He handed her another piece and watched her eat, mindlessly shoving bit after bit into his own mouth.

"Very good," she sighed at the last of it, licking her fingers and leaning back against the tree.

Greg looked up, his eyes sparkling and his lips full and drenched in juice. "You've got a little . . ." He waggled one finger at the corner of his own mouth, frowning as he watched her try to find the bit of pineapple flotsam. "Here, let me."

He leaned forward then, the fingers of his right hand grazing her neck while his thumb flicked away a small bit of pineapple flesh. He was so close that Amanda could feel his breath on her cheek. Then his gaze captured hers and she froze, the breath catching in her throat.

She parted her lips but the words wouldn't come and so she sighed, letting his lips brush hers, letting him share that breath. He lingered there, longer than was proper, not long enough to make her swoon. Then both hands found his chest and she pushed gently. It was a feeble effort but he pulled back just the same, collapsing against the tree opposite hers and frowning at the sand.

"I'm sorry. I don't know what made me do that." He ran both hands through his hair and pressed his palms to his forehead.

Amanda leaped from the ground and took two steps away, gesturing madly with both hands and forcing a smile. "Well, it's not like you have many options . . . here on this island." She stopped, standing dead still with her back to him. She was agitated and her face alight with a rabid blush.

The sound of sand moving met her ears and then he was at her back, a hand on each shoulder, pulling her back against him with enough force to make her heart trip over itself. That warm breath in her ear again, making her head swim, and then he spoke. "If I had a hundred options," he whispered, "I'd still choose you."

A smile pushed her cheeks back into dimples and her eyes sparkled, and no matter how she wanted to spin and let him kiss her again, she couldn't let him see how he had affected her. She pulled away instead, eyes turning up toward the horizon.

"The sun's setting. Do you think we can still make it back before dark?"

He cleared his throat and pocketed his hands. "We only have two choices. We can head for home and end up tromping through the jungle in the dark. Or we can spend the night here and go back in the morning."

She surveyed the sky and thought about it for a moment. "We could always skirt the shoreline."

"That will add miles onto the trip. Besides, it doesn't look like rain. I think we'll be okay sleeping out on the beach tonight."

"At least there's no wild animals." She raised one foot and began rolling the hem of her jeans up to her knee, teetering precariously for a moment before the task was completed. Then she rolled up the other leg and turned to face the water, walking slowly toward the waves.

"What are you doing?" He followed for a few steps but stopped short of actually getting his boots wet.

"I don't know about you, but that pineapple didn't exactly fill me up. I'm going to get us a proper supper." She waded out a few feet, just until the water came level with her pants, then stood stock still, her face locked in concentration. "I used to do this a lot with my dad. Unless sea life is as rare as the animals around here, there should be . . . ah, I think . . . yes!" She bent at the waist shoving her hand into the water for a moment. When she thrust it into the air, it held a large black object.

"We're having rocks for dinner?" His smile was cockeyed and his eyes blinked rapidly.

"Ha ha! Very funny! It's a clam, silly." She tossed it to him and quickly returned to wiggling her toes in the sand.

Greg caught the clam and turned it over in his hand, his face screwed into a mask of concentration. "That's all well and good, but how the hell do we open it? My knife sure isn't up to the task."

"We'll steam them open. You gather some firewood. I'll find us some more clams." She focused on her task for a moment, unaware that he had moved off into the jungle to look for wood. "Do you suppose there are crabs or lobsters around here?" she called over her shoulder.

No answer from Greg. Amanda turned around, shielding her eyes against the gently fading sun. "Greg?"

She waited for a moment, at first expecting an answer, and then praying for it. "Greg!" she hollered, louder and more frantically. She was about to wade back onto shore when something crashed through the brush.

"You okay? You look like you've seen a ghost." His arms were full of firewood and his hat was askew.

"Don't do that!" she spat, frowning at him.

"Do what? I just went to get the firewood like you told me."

"I called to you and you didn't answer. I thought you'd . . . that maybe . . . I was worried is all." She turned back to the task of finding clams, feigning sudden indifference.

"You were worried about me. Admit it." Already he had piled some of the wood into a nice fire pit.

She tossed two more clams onto the shore and shook her head. "You have such an ego!"

Greg stood up from his crouched position by the wood and began to dance around. "Amanda likes Greg! Amanda likes Greg!"

"You knock it off or I'll. . . ." Already, she was making her way back to shore.

"You'll what? Huh? What's a little thing like you going to do to a great big guy like me?" His face was playful, almost childlike.

Amanda reached his position, glaring at him in mock fury. "You'll be sorry, that's what!"

"You better be careful, missy! I know Judo!" He put up his hands, barking and flailing them about.

In an instant, she had his hat off his head and was running down the beach, laughing like a little girl. Her feet kicked up gales of sand as she went and she waved the hat in the air. She glanced back over her shoulder to catch sight of him, hot on her heels and closing in fast. "No, no, no!" She dodged him, running first this way and then that.

The next time she glanced back to see where he was, was her last. He was right behind her then, one arm lashing out to grab the hat, the other arm snatching her off the ground by the waist. She squealed as her feet left the ground, eyes wide and mouth open in a half-laugh, half-yell.

But gravity got the best of them and as Greg spun, the momentum carried them both straight onto the sand. Hat still in one fist, Greg twisted to one side, putting himself between Amanda and the ground, letting her fall on top of him.

They tussled for a moment, each trying to gain control of the hat. In the end, Amanda sat on his chest and grabbed the hat out of his closed fist, spinning and making a mad dive for freedom.

"Oh no you don't!"

Greg rolled just in time to grab one ankle, stopping her long enough to roll on top of her and seize her wrist. "Let go of the hat," he warned in a mock growl.

"No way, Jose!" she laughed, trying to squirm free.

Like a flash, his hands were on her ribs, tickling her until she lay breathless on the ground. The hat slipped from her weakened grasp and still Greg's weight pressed her into the sand. Their clothes were damp and covered in sand, their hair matted with it. And as she lay there, looking up at him, she thought he was the most strikingly handsome man she had ever met. God help her, she wanted him to kiss her again.

And kiss her he did, with as much passion as he could muster. His lips smothered hers, stealing her breath and quickening her already speeding heart. She melted into it, letting his body settle on hers with all its might. He tossed the hat away then, letting the fingers of both hands tangle in her hair, drawing her in, stealing her soul. Current raced over her skin as she realized how deeply she craved him, how desperate she had been for this very moment. The epiphany brought a small cry as she pulled back.

When he withdrew, she felt the burn of tears at the corners of her eyes. Something inside her had snapped, something she'd thought dead since the moment she had last kissed Scott. She wanted Greg then, wanted him in ways she couldn't even begin to fathom.

The tide had risen enough that the waves lapped at them now. Whatever happened between them here was just between them; no one would ever know. There was no escaping the fact that she felt guilty, however, as though she were betraying Scott. In a panic, Amanda shoved Greg aside, letting him fall back onto the sand in a confused and panting heap. And she ran for the water, in part to clean up, in part because he couldn't see her tears if they were mixed with salt water.

And as the water washed up over her hips, she let it cool the fire inside.

CHAPTER FIVE

The night had brought on high humidity and dew had gathered on the leaves and fronds. As the sun rose, the trees wept, releasing small droplets which fell on Amanda's cheek and arm. She lay curled in the grass beneath the tree, head resting on one crooked arm and eyelashes fluttering.

Several feet away, Greg lay beneath his own tree, pretending to sleep as he watched her peaceful face.

It had taken several hours for Amanda to drop off. Her head had been filled with thoughts of Greg and of home. Over and again, she replayed their kiss on a screen of closed lids, her heart speeding each time his lips had touched hers. Even she could see the change in herself, the quick rush of good humor and confidence that had come over her since landing on the island.

Suddenly, Amanda shot bolt upright in the sand, her eyes flying open and her lips parting to spit out a single word. "Birds!"

"What?" She hadn't even been aware of how close Greg had been, but her eyes shot to him now, blinking away sleep and trying to focus. He was propped on his elbows, his shirt unbuttoned and his face marked with the creases of his sleeve.

"I hear birds. Listen."

Greg sat still for a moment, head cocked to one side, taking in the sounds. "You're right."

She listened for a moment longer, a smile claiming her face as the songs of hundreds of birds filled the jungle around her. Then she made her way to her feet, stretching out the kinks and rubbing her neck. "They've come back. The birds have come back."

"But why?" Greg was at her side now, eyes shielded with one hand as he surveyed the treetops.

"Whatever scared them off is gone?" She looked up at him, checking his face to see if she was making sense. "Maybe it was that . . . thing . . . whatever brought me here. Maybe the animals sensed it or saw it and fled."

"Or maybe it's just time for them to migrate." He smiled at her, a nearly sweet gesture, if not for the mocking glint in his eye.

"Well, maybe. But I doubt it. I think that thing scared them and now it's gone, so they've come home. And we'd better keep an eye on our animal friends. If they leave again, it might just mean that that thing is coming back. We have to be ready."

"I'll tell you what I'm ready for. Breakfast. Anybody for a little pineapple?"

"In a minute. But first I have to . . ." She waved one hand toward the jungle, blushing and scratching her head.

Greg nodded in return. "Ladies first." He swept one hand in a grand, bowing gesture toward the brush and smiled.

Amanda lowered her eyes and marched off without another word, her lower lip caught in the vice of her teeth.

Greg watched her go; Amanda felt the heat of his gaze for long moments after she disappeared into the brush. Not five minutes passed before a scream ripped through the still air, sending a cloud of multi-hued birds into the sky from the shock of it.

Greg bolted through the bushes, mindless of the branches and stickers which tore at his clothes. When he hauled himself up short in the clearing, Amanda was huddled in a small ball behind a rock, her head covered with both arms.

Before her, a monkey leaped and screeched, pounding his chest for good measure and baring his teeth. Greg uttered a barely audible, "Christ!" and rubbed his chin.

"Make it go away! God! Do something!" She had raised her head just enough that she could peek out from under one arm. Her eyes were wide and her face looked stricken. Clearly, the monkey had been more of a fright to her than discovering she had been transported into another era.

"Okay." He paused, looking about as if he were searching for something he'd lost. Then he moved a step to the right and grabbed a large branch which had fallen to the ground. Raising it like a baseball bat, he yelled and charged the money.

The ape turned in place, teeth suddenly hidden behind fat lips. It wasn't very large, certainly no match for a trained soldier. But it held its ground for several brave seconds before it gave out one last shriek and ran off into the bushes.

Greg watched it go, the branch still clutched tightly in his hands. Slowly it sagged to his side, and then fell to the ground. "You can come out now."

Amanda lifted her head, surveyed as much of the area as she could from her crouched position. Then she stood slowly, obviously still shaken and very wobbly on her legs. Once she had achieved a full standing position, she side-stepped the rock and flung herself at Greg, arms tightening around his neck as she buried her face in his chest. "Thank you. Thank you so much! I thought sure that thing was going to have me for breakfast."

"It was a monkey, Amanda. It eats fruit. Not pretty girls." Still, he offered what comfort he could, smiling to himself as he rubbed her back and smoothed back her disheveled hair.

Amanda lifted her head from his chest and looked up at him, eyes still a bit too wide for comfort. "You just never know. I mean, did you see how crazed that thing was? What do you suppose made it go off like that?"

Greg shrugged and pulled away. "I'm sure I don't know."

There was a hidden message in that last; Amanda knew it. Somehow, she had put him off by rejecting his advances. Her face darkened and wide eyes turned to a squint. "Well, I just hope it doesn't come back. Anyway, I'll leave you to your business."

She turned in an instant and marched away, her face hot and her hands still curled into fists. More than anything, she wanted to explain. She wanted him to know that it hadn't been because of him that she'd retreated. It had been because of her.

In Greg's absence, she paced the beach and tried to come up with a good, clear way of explaining how she felt. In the end, she dove into the waves, trying to wash the thin coating of sand from her skin and hair. By the time he returned, her urge for discussion had been squashed and any hopes of explaining herself were a distant memory.

"I think we should eat a little something and then head back to the cave. I promised you we'd be ready if and when that thing came back here and it's a promise I intend to keep."

She rung out her hair and then straightened to look at him. "You have a way of fixing the boat?"

"Sort of." Greg lowered himself to the sand and placed a pineapple on the rock before him. "You've seen the sap hardening on those scrawny trees in the jungle?" He looked up to see if she was listening. She nodded. "It gets hard as a rock. So, the way I figure it, all we need is a framework, a backing of some sort. And we can coat the entire hole with that sap and let it harden. What do you think?"

She mulled this over for a minute, her face contorted with the effort. Then she cocked her head to one side and peered at him through a lock of wet hair. "Well, it sounds feasible. But that still won't make the engine work. And how do I get out to the thing if the engine doesn't work?"

"The engine doesn't work because salt water got into it. I'm not an expert in boat motors, especially the kind that come from the future . . ."

"Actually, this boat came from . . . well . . . about now. My father had it most of his adult life."

"Well, then, as I was saying, all we need to do is ignite the first spark in the engine and it should be a go."

"That's wonderful! And even if we can't catch a ride on the Time Warp Express, at least we can get off this island." Her face brightened then, a smile snapping into place.

"Exactly! Because what could possibly be worse than being stuck on an island with me?"

The smile ran away from her face then and her eyes darkened. The remark had been biting, yes, but it was not unwarranted, at least not from where Greg stood. She had to make him understand before it was too late. As it was, he was certain that she hated him, found him repulsive. Even if nothing ever came of it, she couldn't leave him with that feeling.

Amanda reached out and placed her hand on top of his, staying the knife on its journey through the pineapple and drawing his gaze to hers. For a moment, she nearly pulled back, almost lost the nerve to say what so desperately needed to be said. But she cleared her throat and pressed on.

"I need to be frank."

He flashed a smile at her. It was brief and slight, but the humor in it couldn't be missed. "Sure, Frank. Go right ahead."

She returned the smile, flashing him a sneer, briefly and from the corner of her eye. "I just need to tell you why I. . . ." She drew in a deep breath and stared at the ground, her hand drawing instinctively away from his and joining its companion on her lap. "You need to know why nothing happened last night."

"Oh, I know why. And it's okay. Really. I had no right in the world to expect a gorgeous lady like you to fall for a big lummox like me."

"Greg no! God! That's not it at all." She dry swallowed and rocked forward onto her knees. "You're handsome and smart and funny and everything in the world a girl could want."

"Uh huh." He laid out the pineapple on the plate of a leaf and took a piece for himself. "That's why you shoved me into the sand."

"No. It's not. I shoved you into the sand because I'm scared."

"You know what your problem is, Frank? You're not a risk taker."

She laughed at that, and then slid a piece of pineapple into her mouth, pausing only long enough to chew it. "No, I'm not. And is there any wonder? I mean, I take my first big risk and look what happens! I end up sixty years in the past with a man who thinks I hate his guts. Possibly captured by the Japanese. Possibly never to see my home or friends again."

"Everything has its downside, Frank. But mostly it's worth taking the risks. Not everybody gets whisked back in time."

"Please don't call me Frank." He nodded, but she was sure that wasn't the end of it. "What I wanted to tell you is that I was scared. Am scared. You see, it's been a long time since I was with Scott. And when I was with Scott, I was never really with Scott, if you know what I mean."

"I do." He continued to eat, as though listening to a particularly boring poetry recitation or the opera, seemingly unaffected by any of it.

"See, I've never really been with a man before." That one small admission—a common revelation for most—made her face blaze with crimson fury. "And that's why . . ."

"Never?"

"Not ever." She shook her head vehemently, the rabid blush fading to a soft pink.

"But you and Scott were engaged. I just assumed . . ." His face had softened so much. Gone was the stoic soldier mask he had worn so well just a few minutes ago. Once more, he was the boyish, painfully sexy man she had kissed the night before.

"By the time Scott and I realized we were serious enough for . . . for that . . . we decided to save it for our wedding night."

Greg nodded and for a moment, even he looked sad. After a too-long pause, he lifted his eyes and blinked at her. "Tell me something. If you had it to do over again, knowing that Scott wouldn't make it to your wedding night, would you have?"

Her voice, barely above a whisper, cracked. "In a heartbeat."

He nodded slightly, kept his head down as he ate. "That's all I needed to know." He stood and began wiping his hands franticly on his slacks. "If you don't get back home, you'll meet up with Scott again. You will get that second chance."

"And I'll be an old woman by then."

"Still . . ." He wrung his hands furiously and turned toward the water. "I'm going to wash some of this off and then I think we should head home."

She watched him go, her heart sinking fast. A chance had come and gone. And if she had read Greg right, it would not come again. Somehow, that thought made her feel worse than the fact that she had passed up her one chance with Scott. It was painful.

Her gaze followed him as he walked to the water's edge, stripping off his shirt and boots before letting the water devour his half-bare form. She wondered then why it was necessary for him to climb into the water just to wash off a bit of pineapple juice. She wondered as well whether there might be some other reason for his chilled swim. The moment the thought entered her mind, she buried her face in her hands, half ashamed and half proud. But the thought gave her a glimmer of hope and a glimmer was all she needed.

Within moments, Greg was back on shore, his shirt thrown hastily over his arms and his pants dripping into his boots. Amanda righted herself without looking him directly in the eye, and then headed off into the jungle.

The jungle was filled with the sounds of birds and wildlife. Somewhere behind them and then above, Amanda heard the monkey crash through the brush, following them from a safe distance.

She wasn't sure why they had piqued its interest, but she played tag with it all the way home, always trying to catch a clear glimpse of it before it slipped into the brush again.

The familiar cave was just as they had left it, proving to Amanda that there were no enemy troops on the island, waiting to ambush them or ransack their meager belongings. Still, the idea was lodged in the back of her mind that they could appear at any moment, take her captive, and torture her for years to come. God, how she wished Greg had at least had a sidearm with him!

"I'm going down to the beach and get started on that boat," he said out of nowhere.

Amanda turned and gaped at him, mind spinning around possible responses and landing on none. "Would you like some help?" she asked at last.

"I think I can handle it." And with that, he turned and was gone.

Amanda looked after him for a long while, her shoulders drooping noticeably and her eyes darkening. At length, she turned and went into the cave, placing the gathered fruits on the piece of bowed wood at the center of their makeshift home. There was little to do on the island save for gathering food and watching for passing boats. She figured she could do both by going down to the beach. She could be near Greg as well, perhaps find a way to get back in his good graces.

The dry leaves crackled beneath her feet as she walked, once more making her wish for shoes. It was nearly noon and the sand was hot against her skin. She set foot onto the beach delicately, letting her bare feet adjust to the change in texture and temperature.

Greg was already hard at work on the boat. He had pulled a few boards from the bench seats and was using a small tack hammer and rescued nails to put them in place. Amanda spared him only a passing glance as she headed for the water. She couldn't let him think that she'd come down there just to be near him, even if it was the truth. Instead, she rolled up her pants legs and waded into the warm water, toes searching through the sand for oysters, clams, whatever she might find to eat.

As she worked, she wondered if Greg was watching her. Was he still angry over the rejection or had he calmed down? Somehow, she thought that his hurt pride might never heal and that that one moment of rejection might well have ended her chances with him forever. Still, she had to try. She wasn't sure when exactly it had happened, but Greg felt like an extension of her now, a thing that had to be re-united with her in order for her to be complete.

Clams were tossed up on shore to a water-filled divot in the sand for safekeeping until she was ready for them. Once, as she bent to pick up a clam, she turned just so and cast a glance over her shoulder to where Greg was working. There he stood, hammer dangling uselessly in his hand, his eyes unblinking and locked on her form. Amanda smiled.

Deep inside her left pocket, there was a length of twine she had saved from the removal of the boat's seat cushions. She fished it out carefully, struggling against tight pants and wet hands to bring the thing into the light. In her right pocket was a paperclip and she pulled this out as well. The clams had been lying in the manmade tidal pool for some time, heating in the sun and opening from the heat. She opened one and wrenched the flesh from the shell, piercing the clam with the paperclip and using that to drag the twine through the creature.

"Sorry, but a girl's gotta eat, you know?"

She saved the shells in a small pile, just in case they might have use of them later. Then she tied the twine in a knot and tossed the tethered clam into the ocean as far as it would go. Behind her, hammering began and stopped, telling her that Greg was as fascinated with her as she had wanted him to be.

Slowly, she reeled the clam in, letting it drag along the bottom and feeling for resistance as it went. After several minutes, the clam was at her feet and she stooped to pick it up and toss it back into the sea.

A shadow fell over her shoulder and her head snapped to the side, eyes boring into Greg's as she fought to still her heart from the sudden shock.

"What are you doing with that thing?" A cockeyed smile crinkled the corner of his mouth as he spoke.

"Catching crabs. My dad taught me this, though we used chicken necks instead. I'm hoping crabs like clams as much as they like chicken necks."

He nodded briefly and watched, face tightening into a grimace as she worked the twine. "And what will you do when the crab finally does follow the clam up here?"

She turned a frown on him and sighed. "Back home, we teased the crab over a net and Daddy snapped it up. I'm not sure what to do now." She thought hard for a moment and then her face lit up. "If it's still there, Daddy always kept a fishing net in the back locker."

Greg smiled and mock saluted. "I'll see if it's still there." He turned and trotted toward the boat, getting no more than five feet before being startled to a halt by her cry.

"I've got one! Hurry!"

In a flash, Greg was back at her side, the net spinning in his hand and his eyes twinkling. "You lucked out. It was still there."

"That's my dad. Always a creature of habit. Now, just lay it down in the sand and wait until I get the crab over it. But be quiet. They scare easily."

Greg tiptoed to the water's edge and placed the net in the sand, making sure that his shadow didn't fall over it as he stooped to watch for the crab's approach. Within a few minutes, the end of the string with the clam on it came into view, the crab's large claw clamped onto the clam. It teetered along after the clam, snapping and pulling at it, trying to claim the meal. And then Greg snapped the net up into the air.

"Woo hoo! I got him! I got him!" Greg held the net high in the air, the crab flailing its claws uselessly and the net spraying droplets of water into their faces. Still, Greg danced around like he'd just found his first gold nugget in the Colorado River.

"Good job! Just look at him!" Amanda reeled in the twine as she approached the net to have a closer look.

"He's no King Crab, but he sure is better than nuts and berries." Greg looked between crab and woman, his face alight with good humor and joy. "Now what?"

"Well," Amanda began, glancing hurriedly around, "we need something to put him in. I wish we had a bucket or something."

"How about a plastic container? Will that do?"

"I guess it'll have to." She took the net as it was shoved into her hands, watching Greg dart away and smiling for all she was worth. "I'm guessing we can easily catch about a dozen of these guys in pretty short order. We'll eat well tonight."

Greg returned with a Rubbermaid plastic container. He partially filled it with water, and then took the net from Amanda's wet hands. "Now, if we could just find a cow and a butter churn, we'd eat like kings." He laughed at that, bending quickly to deposit the crab into the plastic container.

"Be careful. Try to pick him up by his back legs and don't get close to his claws. Daddy made that mistake once and the darn thing held on until he finally smashed it to pieces with his boot."

Greg simply grabbed a bit of the net's bottom, then flipped the whole affair upside down over the container and let the crab drop into its new home. "Let's get some more," he laughed, thrusting the net out to her. "Only this time, I do the baiting and you do the catching."

"Deal."

She returned his bright smile and took the net. It felt good to be the source of his smiles rather than his sorrow.

They took turns with the twine, replacing the clam as needed and tossing crabs into the plastic container until they figured they had enough. Then they put the lid on and Greg carried it further onto the beach, setting it down in the shade and wiping his hands against his jeans in a feeble effort to remove the clam juice which had coated them.

"This is going to be so amazing, after all this time on fruits and nuts. Lady, you're a genius and I think I love you!" He grabbed her face in both hands and gave her a rough, noisy smack on the lips. "I'll get the firewood and we can cook these critters."

For the first time in her life, Amanda didn't blush. The excitement of the moment infected her, lighting her face and drawing out a long laugh. By the time Greg had gone and her laughter had subsided, she realized that her heart had tripled its speed and her face was hot, not with a rabid blush but with genuine heat.

Greg returned just in time to stop her from fully realizing her need for him. He squatted down to lay out the fire as she watched, her eyes drizzling over him, memorizing every single square inch of his broad back and rippling arms.

"It's kind of mean, don't you think, to just put them on a fire." Her voice was soft and far away, as though she was speaking through the veil of a dream.

"Oh, don't you dare get all soft on me! We need to eat and they're . . . well . . . they're food." His face was caught somewhere between panic and frustration. It made her smile.

"Don't get me wrong. I fully intend to eat them. But just casting them onto a fire seems awfully cruel."

Greg nodded slowly, looking from crabs to fire and back again. Hands on his hips, he gazed directly into her eyes, his face a study in solemn resolution. "I'll tell you what, you go take a swim and I'll cook the crabs. They don't scream so you'll never have to know a thing about it until you're elbow-deep in crab meat."

Her face flashed to a smile and just then, she wanted to kiss him more than she wanted to breathe. For just a second, she could actually feel his lips on hers, his warm breath dancing over her cheek. She paused for a moment, realizing quite suddenly that her chest was heaving and her heart was pounding again.

She took one step forward, her tongue grazing over her lips to moisten them. The taste of sea water and sweat filled her mouth and for a moment she nearly drew back. But her body ached to share his breath and the need for it filled her head. In an instant, before she could talk herself out of it, her hand was at the back of his neck and her lips were crushed to his.

A shudder wracked her body as she felt his hands wander over her back. He pulled her in close, a little moan escaping as his lips parted to let his tongue dance with hers. Eyes clamped tightly shut, her body pressed to his, tiny sparks of light danced behind her lids and her head swam from the heat.

Her breath was lost to her then, lost in the desperate need and the current that danced over her skin. She would breathe again once he released her . . . if he released her. It didn't matter. He was like the air to her now.

CHAPTER SIX

His lips parted from hers but the heat lingered, nearly making her stutter in the face of all that rampant desire. She blinked twice and cleared her throat, noting so clearly the confusion on Greg's own gaping face. Then she tugged twice on his shirt and winked at him. "Don't burn the crabs," she whispered and scampered off toward the water.

She'd have given anything to have turned and studied his face just then. She wanted to gauge the need and confusion in his eyes. But she couldn't let him know how deeply that kiss had affected her; she just couldn't. Instead, she dove headlong into the waves and swam only as far as she could and still touch the bottom. Only then did she turn and by then Greg had returned to the crabs and the fire.

The water was warm against her skin, still trapped beneath her clothes and steaming from their kiss. She had grown used to wearing clothes to swim and just as used to wearing the clothes until they dried. It kept her cooler longer in the tropical heat and kept her from getting sunburned.

She dove for a while, looking for pretty fish and chasing waves. The next time she surfaced and checked the shore, Greg waved her in. Slowly, she walked toward the shore, wringing the water from her hair and letting the droplets fall from her clothes as she moved toward him.

"Dinner is served," he laughed, sweeping his arm in the direction of a large pile of cooked crabs.

With the use of his knife and several small stones, they cracked the crabs and ate in silence. There was no talk of the kiss; no furtive glances cut across the distance between them. The event was marked only by occasional groans of pleasure and the cracking of shells.

When all the crab had been devoured and all that remained was a pile of vacant shells and the oily residue that ran down their arms, Greg rose and stretched and looked out to sea.

"I don't know about you, but I really don't think I'll be getting much done for the rest of the evening."

"The sun's going to set soon anyway. I say we go back to the cave and take a nice long nap." Amanda brushed her hands against her jeans and stood. Behind her, something moved in the bushes. She spun toward the sound, nearly releasing a cry until she caught sight of a monkey's tail disappearing into the brush.

"I'll clean up this mess and stow the tools in the boat. If the weather's good tomorrow, I'll put the last two boards on and we can begin coating it with the sap."

Amanda nodded slowly, staring into his soft eyes as the sensation of that kiss returned to her lips. Suddenly, her focus shifted and she found her gaze locked on his full lips, the heat spreading through her again.

"Hello?"

Amanda snapped back to reality, blinking rapidly and stammering for a moment. "What?"

"I said that you could collect the sap while I apply it. Even in this heat, it won't stay liquid long and it has to be spread right before it hardens."

"Oh, sure. Fine. We'll get it done no problem." She was still dazed, though she hoped he didn't know why.

"You pick up after dinner. I'll pick up the tools. Then we can head home."

Again, she nodded and blinked stupidly. "Home."

Suddenly, she was in a rush to clean up and get home. The sun would go down soon and there would be nothing left to do but lie down in the cave and. . . .

She gathered the shells hurriedly into the makeshift sack of her shirt hem and dumped them on the fire, which she then extinguished with a good dose of sand. Then she filled in the hole and dusted off her hands, turning to watch Greg at his own work.

He was taller than Scott had been and far more muscular. He

was just more . . . physical. The memory of his grip on her during that kiss was still so fresh that it brought a new rash of goose bumps to her arms when she thought of it.

"Need some help?" she called to him, hoping to break the spell those memories had cast over her.

"All done," he exclaimed, throwing up his hands and smiling. "Let's head for home."

Already, the sun had slipped closer to the horizon. It would be dark within the hour and anything other than sleep would be an impossibility. Greg held out his hand and she took it, letting her fingers lace with his as though they'd done so a hundred times before. One touch and she was on fire again, her eyes turned away so he wouldn't see, her lips tightly pursed so as to not release that gasp of excitement.

The monkey was still nearby, watching them. She wasn't sure why he watched. Perhaps there were no other monkeys about and he was wanting for companionship. She wasn't really afraid of it anymore, merely curious as the monkey must have been. Still, she used the noise as an excuse to edge closer to Greg and hurry him along toward home.

By the time they reached the cave, the sun had disappeared beneath the horizon line and long shadows reached snake-like fingers across the ground toward them. The wind had all but died and the temperature had dropped to a tolerable level. Still, the air was thick with moisture and their skin had beaded with sweat. Amanda glanced up at the cave, then back to the inviting pool of water before it.

"If it's all the same to you, I'd like to wash up real quick." She offered up her sweetest smile, as though he should have caught the full meaning of that statement.

"Sure thing." He said that and nothing more. Neither did he make a move toward the cave.

Amanda blinked at him for a few beats, her smile widening as she waited. Finally, she let loose a little giggle and shook her head. "Would you mind giving me a little privacy?"

It was Greg's turn to blush. "Sorry, sorry, sorry," he blurted, rapid-fire. "I'll be inside if you need me."

Amanda watched him go, his head hung low and his eyes on the ground. "If only you knew," she whispered only to herself.

Once he was safely inside the cave, view obstructed behind a curtain of water, she peeled off her clothes. The moon was full and it lit the water like the silver back of a mirror. She let the water swallow her whole, slipping beneath its surface and sending out ripples as she moved. From beneath the water, the moon looked like a freshly painted canvas, left out in the rain, the paint running toward its bottom. She skimmed the surface long enough to catch a breath, then dove once more.

Once she was thoroughly wet, Amanda stood to her full height, still waist-deep in the water. With the heel of one hand she scrubbed at her skin, wishing with all her heart that she had even one bar of that rose-scented soap she had kept on hand for special occasions.

Scarcely a sound disturbed the silence until a loud splash echoed through the jungle, sending birds into the air and drawing a quick scream from Amanda's throat. Before she could make a move toward shore, the water began to ripple as something moved toward her at a steady clip.

Then he was there, breaking cleanly through the surface of the water so close to her that his chest nearly brushed hers. Instinctively, she let herself squat down, letting the water swallow her almost to the shoulders. Her hands went to her mouth and she held her breath. In her mind's eye, she could see the beat of her heart—fast and furious—making ripples in the water, sending them out like radio waves. The water immediately around her began to heat and the least little movement brought her in contact with cooler water, making her shiver.

The moment froze in time as his face came even with hers, eyes shimmering just inches away. Then his hands were on her, pulling her close. Every nerve ending screamed as her flesh met his, his lips descending, hovering, teasing. Already his hand had found the mane of her hair, was clutching. He had complete control.

"Miss Amanda," he whispered, his voice husky and full of desire, "I think I'm falling in love with you."

And then that longed-for embrace stole her breath. His hands clutched at her and she felt his need. A moan escaped her lips and when her breath returned, she was panting against his cheek. She couldn't stop. She was desperate, ready to explode. Every inch of her trembled closer to him.

He withdrew all too soon, his hands finding her face, brushing back the hair that clung to her wet skin, thumbs stroking her cheeks. She was in full blush now, could feel it from the top of her head to the tips of her toes. He kissed her forehead, nose, both eyes, her lips. And all the while his need was trapped between them, pressing her, stoking her own flames.

He leaned in again, pressing his forehead to hers and smiling. "I swear to you, if there was any way I could carry you to the cave, this would be the most romantic moment of your life." He let loose a boyish laugh, such a sorrowful, boy-like grin.

If you had ever asked her at what point she had decided to make love to him, she could not have told you. But the decision had been made and the decision had set her free. She rose fully from the water then, pulling back from him but taking his hand for good measure. Unashamed, unabashed, she walked toward the shore with Greg in tow. There would be sand between their toes, they were soaking wet, but none of that mattered.

He followed her to the cave, clothes forgotten on the tiny beach by the pond, and they lay down upon the pushed-together makeshift beds. She should have been nervous, but she wasn't. She should have been scared, but her heart was jubilant. He was so slow, so gentle and tender; each touch made her want him more. And when the moment was right—that one perfect, Heaven-sent moment—two became one.

Sunlight found them that next morning. It crept on them like a thief and stole the night. Amanda pulled his arm more tightly around her, hugged it, smiled to herself and no one else. She felt him pressed hard against her back, spooning her. Realization found her and she rolled over to meet him. "Good morning," she chirped, smiling at him, brushing the back of one hand along his cheek.

"Good morning, beautiful." He kissed the tip of her nose, let his hand run the width and length of her flat stomach. He stroked the hair back from her eyes, let his lips rest on hers for a moment. "Last night was so . . ." He trailed off in a growl, his forehead coming to rest on hers, infecting her with his blush.

"Yea, it was." She giggled and hugged him, pulling back from him and smiling. "Is it okay if I have dibs?"

"Yea. I'll come down and gather some breakfast. You go on ahead."

She stood, so painfully aware that he was watching her, trying to be casual and calm. But it made her so nervous that she nearly tripped on the first step out of the cave. He waited until she was on the ground and turned away before he began his descent.

Her clothes were in a heap by the pond and she grabbed them on her way to the toilet area. She smiled as she walked, completely unable to wipe that bit of evidence from her face. It was a beautiful day in a glorious place and the very handsome and well-muscled man in that cave was hers and hers alone.

She completed her ablutions and dressed herself, running her fingers through her hair and trying to straighten it as best she could. She was on her way back to the pond when the monkey made its presence known. The sound of it crashing through the bushes was inescapable and at one point, she heard him race ahead of her. Then suddenly, as she was about to break into the clearing, the monkey dropped down from the tree right in front of her. He hung from a branch by one leg and one arm, swinging and taunting her.

She came to a dead stop and stared at him, caught between fear and laughter. Obviously, he meant her no harm or he would have attacked her by now. Slowly, she walked over to him and as she stepped just beneath the spot where he hung, he dropped from the tree, spinning and grabbing her shoulders as he fell. The force of it nearly toppled her, but she managed, through several stumbling steps backward, to save them.

The monkey chirped happily at her, making faces and holding onto her with all four limbs. Instinctively, she wrapped her arms around him, helping to support him. His eyes were bright and he seemed well-acclimated to humans for some reason. He made her laugh.

"I have no idea where you came from, but I guess you're part of our tribe now. Let's go get some breakfast, eh?"

He seemed content to ride in Amanda's arms all the way back to the pond. As they broke into the open, Greg stood to gawp at them, his dropped jaw turning into a laugh as he watched the monkey's antics.

"Who's your little friend there?" he chuckled.

"He literally dropped into my arms. I'm going to call him 'Cheetah' and I think I shall make him my minion."

"Minion, huh?"

"He can be very useful. He can get to the coconuts in the tall trees. He can probably break them open more easily than we can too. Chimpanzees are very strong."

"I see. Well, good luck teaching him to get the fruit without eating it." Greg reached out a hand and stroked Cheetah's head. The chimpanzee transferred from woman to man, hugging Greg's neck. "But why the name 'Cheetah' for a monkey?"

"Didn't you ever see the Tarzan movies? The monkey in them is named 'Cheetah.' "

"Okay, no. I haven't seen the movies. But you can call him whatever you want. Now, if you'll hold your minion, I'm going to go take care of business."

She giggled as he handed the chimp to her, pecked her on the lips, and headed off to the toilet area.

Nearby, there was a palm tree of the very tall and very straight variety. While it had shed two coconuts, the top of the tree was festooned with huge clumps of the ripe fruits. Amanda leaned back, shading her eyes from the glaring sun and wondering silently whether even the chimp could make it to the top. And if he did, could he make it back down with the coconut in hand?

She stooped to pick up one of the cast-off coconuts, rolling it over in her hands and squatting to meet the chimp's gaze. "I doubt that you eat these," she started with a smile. "We eat these. But we can't reach them." She pointed to the coconut and then the top of the tree. "Go get them. Get the coconut. Go up there and get the coconut."

Monkey brains being what they are, Cheetah stared at her for a moment. Then he looked at the coconut in her hand, to the tree, then back to her face. In one fluid motion, he grabbed the coconut from her hand and raced up the tree with it tucked neatly under one arm. He had no trouble taking the tree with his three remaining limbs and when he reached the top, he hung there, holding out the coconut like a trophy.

She giggled and shook her head. "Not exactly what I had in

mind, pal. Throw me the coconut." She held out her hands, ready to catch it. "Toss it here. Give it here. Drop it. Oh, what's your trigger?"

Apparently, "drop it" was his trigger, for he released the coconut without warning, watching as it dropped and gathered speed. Amanda experienced a moment of panic when she realized just how hard that coconut was going to hit her hands. Still, she was able to catch it with something akin to coordination, if not actual coordination. Then she set it on the ground and looked back to Cheetah.

"Good boy! That was very good. Now, throw me another. Drop the coconut. Drop one. Drop it. Give me the coconuts."

And all he did was stare. He must have thought her daft, asking him to throw a coconut which he had already thrown. Humans were so stupid, after all. They couldn't even get their own coconuts.

"Get the coconut. Get the coconut!" she shouted, ever more excited, jumping with each repetition.

The chimp finally caught on, grabbing a coconut and releasing his grip on the tree. He swung from the coconut and for a moment, Amanda thought she would have to catch both coconut and chimp. But then he wrapped his legs around the trunk once more and gave the thing a mighty yank. The coconut came loose in his hand and he held it aloft for a second before tossing it at her.

Amanda watched carefully, gauging the distance and trying hard to calculate its speed. When she had played baseball in high school, she had always played outfield. And when the ball had actually finally come her way, she had put her glove in front of her face and ducked. So, it took a great screwing-up of her courage to face that falling coconut, catch it, and not fall down.

"Oh, good boy! Good boy, Cheetah!" She was laughing now and clapping her hands.

Cheetah sang out his joy, bellowing a mighty chimpanzee song and thumping his chest. And then he grabbed another coconut and tossed it down. Amanda wasn't quite ready for that one, but she adapted, putting her hands up at the last minute and catching it only by the skin of her teeth. Then the chimp grabbed another coconut and threw it.

He began grabbing coconuts from the tree and throwing them in rapid-fire secession, grunting and calling to her. At one point, he grabbed quite a few, then threw them in a barrage at her. The game was afoot and he was loving it.

Amanda did the best she could to catch them, but it was like juggling plates. They came too fast and were too widely spread in their trajectories. She screamed then, running from the tree and the coconuts and the insane chimp, all the time yelling, "Stop it! Stop! Stop!"

Greg came into the clearing just in time to see Amanda duck and cover her head as she fled the tree. For some reason not immediately clear to Amanda, he found it the funniest thing he had ever seen. He bent over with laughter, his face red with the effort and tears streaming down his cheeks. She glared at him as she ran past, swerving to hide behind him, clutching his shoulders as he shook with laughter.

"Relax," he laughed. "He has to run out of coconuts eventually."

She punched him in the shoulder then, actually making him flinch and duck. It was very satisfying. "It's not funny! Those things hurt!"

He hugged her then, soothing away her anger with a kiss, though he was still fighting hysteria. Meanwhile, Cheetah realized that the girl and the man were no longer playing his game. He stopped and shimmied down the tree trunk, waiting at their feet for them to stop whatever they were doing and pay attention to him.

"I think from now on we'll stick with mangoes or papayas. They hurt less." She rubbed her head for effect and smiled.

"That might be a good idea. Come on. Let's eat breakfast. I want to get working on that boat of yours. We should be ready in case that thing shows up again."

That last stopped her in her tracks. What had he meant by that? That he was going with her? Or that he intended for her to go alone? Why had he not assumed or asked or even begged for her to stay? A pall fell over her as she sat down. Had last night been nothing to him? A dalliance?

She picked up a mango and dug her thumbnail beneath the skin, pulling it back and handing it to Cheetah. Then she peeled one for herself and bit into it. When she had swallowed, she said softly, "Come with me."

Greg looked up then, his face taut, his usually handsome features sharp and dark. "What?"

"Come with me. Back to my time." She looked at him hopefully, tried to smile.

"We don't even know that I can. I mean, maybe you can only pass through in the exact same way that you came here? What if a second person would throw that off? We just don't know anything about it."

"And so we don't know that you can't come. Please. Greg, I don't want to lose you." She stopped short of saying those three words that she longed to say. It was too soon. He would think her a fool.

He scooted closer to her, took her hand in his and kissed it longingly, his eyes shut. "And I don't want to lose you either. Stay here. Stay with me."

"I can't. I have a job, a house, friends . . ."

"And I have all that here." He released her hand, his face sad.

"But my time is better. We've cured a dozen diseases. We have TV and the internet and cell phones . . ."

"Those are all things. What people do you have? What people?"

She blinked and thought. Her face was sullen and she felt tears pooling. "I have my friend Dana, and . . . and . . ."

"I have my mother, my best friend, my brother. And I have this war to help fight."

"We win the war, by the way. We win." She frowned and shook her head. "And there's another reason why I can't stay. I'll let loose some information, do something that will screw up the timeline. I could change history. And what happens when we get to the point where I was born? The urge to go tell myself things would be unbearable. I couldn't stop myself from saving Scott. And then that would allow Scott and the other me to get married and then I would cease to be here now . . . I think. Maybe."

She sighed in misery and hung her head. Her sorrow was so all-consuming that she didn't even notice when Greg put his arms around her. He held her for a moment, letting the pain pass, letting her head clear. Then he turned her chin with one finger and smiled.

"We can't figure out the fate of the entire universe. All we can do is make the best decision we can for ourselves. And the best decision for me is to be with you. Here . . . there . . . wherever. But I want to have the boat done and ready in case that thing shows up again. So, let's not worry ourselves about all the things that might happen. Let's enjoy today and worry about making the right things happen."

He kissed her then, long and deep and hot. Her head spun from it and as she pulled back to look into his eyes, she smiled. Just then, she decided that being trapped on that island with Greg for the rest of her life wouldn't be such a bad thing.

CHAPTER SEVEN

The day was long and extraordinarily hot. Since it took two people to catch crabs, Amanda borrowed Greg's knife and used it to whittle the end of a bamboo pole into a sharp point. The animals had begun to return to the island slowly. Bird calls filled the air during the day and twice she heard something crashing through the bushes in front of her. She knew it wasn't Cheetah because he was at her side, so she reasoned that it must be some other sort of wild animal. On the off chance that it was a wild boar, she wanted to be ready to hunt and kill it. The thing would make a fine feast, worthy of a luau.

She completed two spears, then went into the jungle to gather some bananas and papayas for lunch. Greg had been working on the boat all morning, his bare chest tanning to a dark mocha and his muscles bristling with strength. She couldn't help but stare at him as he worked, her mind latching onto the thought that he was hers, she was his. That thought alone brought a smile to her face, warmth to her heart.

"Come have some lunch," she called to him, setting the fruit on the flat rock which had become their table. There was a fire pit to her left, made by the strategic laying of stones. The fire used to cook each meal burned up the remains from the meal before it. It was efficient and ecologically correct.

"I think the boat's almost done," he said as he sat down in the sand. He drew one arm across his forehead, wiping away the sweat which had gathered there. "Next, we have to figure out how to fire that engine. If we can't do that, then we have to find a way to make some oars."

She looked up then, stunned by his use of the plural. Her face brightened, she felt her heart quicken. "Oars? As in more than one?"

Greg smiled, nodded, stuffed a piece of papaya into his mouth. "Yea. Did I fail to mention that? It takes two oars to row a boat. Unless you like going in circles, that is." He paused, let her heart plummet for a moment. "And it takes two people to operate them."

She tackled him, throwing herself across the distance and grabbing his neck. Fruit went flying and sand sprayed up as they hit the ground in a tangle. A rain of kisses fell on his face and she fought to stay atop him. "You're going with me," she said when finally she caught her breath.

He was holding her tightly, stroking her hair, his face so soft and gentle that it melted her heart. "Your time sounds like a much better place. Less disease, no wars. And if I leave here, all future mes will cease to exist. There will be only one and he will be yours."

She couldn't have stopped the tears from falling if her life had depended on it. "I love you so much, Greg. So much it hurts."

"I can take care of that hurt," he said softly, tugging at her jeans.

"Can you now?" She giggled and the sound of it was lewd; a complete surprise to her.

"I can." He locked her in a tight embrace, his hand fumbling for the button of her jeans, now trapped between them.

They made love in the midst of the sand and fallen fruit, the grinding of their bodies creating a rut where they lay. And when they were done, they ran to the water, naked, letting it wash them clean and sooth their hot skin. They frolicked for a while, playing in the waves and relaxing in the shallow water. It was a fine day to live on an island; a fine day to be in love.

Playtime over, Greg returned to his work on the boat and Amanda cast her line in the water, trying to provide them with fish for dinner. There was no stress here, nothing to do but make love, sleep, and hunt for food. One was never far from the other and scarcely fifteen minutes passed before the two would look up simultaneously, smile, and blow a kiss like a couple of teenagers.

Amanda amassed a school of four fish for their dinner, which she cleaned using Greg's knife. They buried the remains in the jungle, not wanting to attract sharks that would scare off further fish. Once she was done with that, she returned to the beach to build their nightly fire. Greg had already completed his work and when she came into the clear, he was squatted by the fire pit, stacking the wood.

"I swear, we eat better now than when I was back home," he chuckled, striking flint against rock and watching the logs.

Amanda sat next to him, wrapping her arms around her bent legs and resting her chin on her knees. "Healthier, anyway. So how is the boat coming along?"

"It's all done. I want the sap to cure for a day. Then I think we should test it to make sure it will hold water before we do any more on it."

She nodded and frowned. "We have no guarantee that that thing, whatever it was, will come back. But I guess we'll be ready if and when it does."

"There's a whole lot we don't know. But worst-case scenario, you get stuck here forever and we never leave the island."

She nodded and sighed. "In the grand scheme of things, that doesn't sound as bad as it did two days ago. I think I can live with it." Then she proffered a smile and a wink.

"Good. Then hand me those fish, woman! Your man has worked up a powerful hunger." It sounded so absurd, even to him, that he was forced to laugh.

They sat in the shade of the little grove of areca palms and cooked and ate the fish. Cheetah, who had been off in the jungle somewhere, joined them for supper. He had brought fists full of bananas, which he offered to share with them. The fish made his nose wrinkle and he moved upwind of the fire so that the smell wouldn't be too strong. But he never strayed far from Amanda as the sun began to set.

Greg turned to offer him a bit of guava, his eyes darting to the two spears stuck in the ground behind them. "What are those?" he asked, nodding toward the spears.

"Oh, I used your knife to whittle spears from two of the bamboo poles I found. Something was crashing through the bushes before and I know it wasn't Cheetah since he was with me. I figured that if it was a boar, we could hunt and kill it. It sure would make for some good eating."

"And if it's something else? A big cat? A Japanese soldier?"

"Then it's better than nothing at all." She frowned then and screwed up her face. "I sure wish we had a gun."

"So do I. I mean, if the war does come to us, we're sitting ducks." He sighed and sat back, letting his eyes wander over things that weren't there. "We do need a plan, though. In case they come."

"Yea." A darkness fell over Amanda then, stealing her sunshine and crooking her mouth. "I guess the best thing to do would be to hide in the cave until they leave."

"Unless there's heavy artillery fire. Then they could cause a cave-in and we'd be trapped."

Her shoulders slumped and her head fell to her knees. "What can we do then?"

"I guess we'll play it by ear. If they come, we'll hide in the cave. But if there's artillery fire, then we'll have to run to the farthest side of the island and hope for the best."

"And if we're captured? What will they do to us then?"

Greg's eyes met hers for the briefest of moments. She looked more worried, more scared than she ever had. "I really don't want to think about that. You're a woman, so it's anybody's guess whether they'll kill you immediately, or keep you as a bargaining chip. But I'm a Navy pilot. They'll want information from me."

"God!" She knew what that meant and it terrified her.

"They may never come here. We don't know. But if they do, the important thing is to not get caught. And if we do get caught, we have to cooperate in every way possible. Don't give them a reason to kill us. Surrender immediately and pray that they honor the Geneva Convention."

"If it's all the same to you, I'll just pray that they don't come." She smiled feebly and stood up. "We should be getting back to the cave. It's almost dark now."

They kicked sand over the fire and grabbed their tools. Neither said a word on the way back to the cave. Cheetah walked beside them, his hand in Amanda's. He seemed to sense her worry. Their beds, permanently pushed together, were waiting for them back at the cave. A long day of hard work had tired them and they fell asleep before goodnights were even said.

In the middle of the night, Amanda awoke in Greg's arms. Her head was on his chest as he breathed slowly. It was warm and she was comfortable, safe, happy. So why, then, had she awoken? She laid there for a few minutes, listening and wondering as to the origins of her sudden rise out of sleep. And then she heard it. A crashing boom, like a car exploding or a bomb going off. That and nothing more.

She sat bolt upright, her breath coming in quick gasps, her body shaking. The suddenness of her movement stunned Greg into wakefulness. He sat up beside her in the dark. The sound of the waterfall kept most of the island noises from ever reaching their ears. But that one, lightning-quick blast had drowned out even the waterfall.

All was silence now, though, as Amanda sat in the dark, listening. Surely, the other shoe would drop soon. There would be another boom.

"What's wrong, honey?" Greg asked into her ear.

The sound of his voice startled her and she jumped. "I heard a sound. A huge, loud boom sound." She had started to tremble and he put his arms around her. She pulled them even tighter around herself.

"I don't hear anything now. Is it possible you were dreaming?"

She shook her head violently, beginning to rise, to walk to the waterfall and look beyond it. The noise came again and she screamed this time, clinging to the wall of the cave for dear life. "Oh God!" she cried softly. "Is that?"

Pulling on his pants and zipping them quickly, he pressed Amanda back against the wall and shushed her. Then he was out the mouth of the cave, standing behind the water and peering beyond it. Lightning split the sky and immediately afterward the earth shook. Outside the waterfall, rain was falling in buckets.

"It's a thunderstorm. That's all. It's okay."

She hurried to his arms then, standing in the safe harbor of them and still trembling as she looked out over their peaceful island. Trees whipped about and leaves flew past. The sky was alight with electricity and the rain fell so hard and fast that you couldn't see the waterfall in the middle of it. "It scared me so bad. I thought . . . I thought . . ."

"But it's not the Japanese. Not the war." He pulled her chin up so that her eyes met his. "It's just a storm and we're still safe."

She nodded quickly and sank back into his arms, still shaking a bit. "Just a storm."

"Come back to bed, honey. Let's try to get some sleep and maybe it'll be over by the time we wake up."

She nodded though he couldn't see her, and felt her way across the cave to their bed. He laid down first, opening his arms for her and engulfing her in them. Each time the thunder shook the island, she grasped at him more tightly, clamping her eyes shut against the lightning and trying to not hear the rain. Eventually, she fell asleep again but that sleep was fitful and wracked with nightmares.

When the sun finally rose and they were awake, it was still raining but the ferocity of the storm had lessened. There was debris all around and about the beach and scattered over the top of their pond. But no significant damage seemed to have been done to the island. As she tended to her needs, Greg went to check the boat, fearing that the waves had further damaged it or that it had been swept out to sea entirely. The rain was light and warm and Amanda didn't so much mind it without its attending thunder and lightning and wind. She wondered briefly where Cheetah went when such storms rolled through.

There was fruit all over the ground and she began gathering it up, realizing after her second armload that she could never hope to save it all from rot. She looked up into the trees, which had been all but stripped of their fruits. They might have to live on just fish and clams for a while, until the fruit grew back.

Greg found her as she was putting her third armload of fruit onto the large flat rock from which they ate. She checked his face, looking for any sign of bad news there. He was dripping from the rain, his shirt in absentia, his chest and arms tightly muscled and broad. She smiled and raised her eyebrows into question marks.

"The boat's fine." He laughed. "I had all sorts of visions of it crushed on the beach or just gone. But it's just fine." He swiped a raindrop from the end of his nose and ran a hand through his hair. "But I do think we should give it another day after the rain stops before we test it."

She nodded and smiled. "Well, I guess another day or two won't hurt. Go do your thing. Breakfast is served." She winked at him and popped a piece of mango into her mouth.

"Be right back." He sauntered off in the direction of their toilet, waving back at her for good measure.

Amanda sat on the wet sand, eating slowly and staring off into the future. She wondered, ever so briefly, what Dana and the others were all doing in her absence. It dawned on her then that that was the first time she had spared a thought for them since the whole ordeal had begun. Did they miss her? Were they searching for her? Had she been fired or her electricity turned off?

Greg's shadow fell over her, shaking her from her reverie. Suddenly, she realized that she didn't really care what was happening in her old life. Her new life was just fine, thank you very much.

They ate what fruit their stomachs could hold, then left the rest on the rock. By that time, the rain had slowed to a slight trickle and the sun was doing battle with the clouds. By noon, the sun had proved its superiority and the rain began to dry.

They hadn't seen a single sign of Cheetah since the storm and Amanda had begun to worry. She and Greg sat at the edge of the pond, feet dangling as they soaked up the sun and silence. Just as she was about to head to the beach for some fishing, there was a sound in the bushes some fifty feet from where they sat. She froze, listening as the sound drew nearer.

"It must be Cheetah," Greg offered softly.

"Ssh!" she said, pulling at his arm.

Through the underbrush, she could hear the shuffling of feet and the breaking of branches. She pulled Greg backward, toward the cave, her eyes riveted on the spot where the branches had begun to move. "Get in the cave," she whispered. "It's not Cheetah."

They turned and hurried then, back to the cave and the safety it offered. She saw nothing of the thing as it meandered through the jungle. She had no idea what it was. From behind the curtain of water, they watched the thing approach until it broke free of the bushes and grass and stood, broad and fat, in the clearing.

"It's a pig," Amanda giggled, her eyes riveted to the thing.

"Wild boar. Nothing like a domestic pig." Greg, too, was watching as he corrected her.

"Whatever. We have to kill it."

He looked at her, his face lost in confusion. "Why?"

"One word: Barbecue." She spun away, reaching for the homemade spears, one of which she passed to Greg.

"Are you seeing those tusks?"

"Yes." Still, she stared at the thing, who had discovered their pile of fruit and had taken to rutting at it, selecting his favorites and eating them with great delight.

"And you expect us to chase that thing down and kill it with a couple of pieces of bamboo?" His voice had gotten louder, his face more serious.

"It worked for the cavemen."

"And how much experience do you have in spear hunting? Or boars?"

"None at all. Come on."

She began her descent from the cave then, as Greg stood and watched, the spear dangling uselessly from his hand and his jaw agape. Quickly, he realized that she would be killed if he didn't help her. Besides, he was the man. It was his job to hunt and gather. So, he made his way down from the cave to stand by her side, hoping against hope that the boar wouldn't see them and simply charge.

"I have no idea what I'm doing," he said. "How does this work?"

"Well, I think one of us should circle around behind him, get ready to spear him when the other person scares him in that direction."

"Or get speared with those tusks. He's going to be panicked when he runs. I don't want to get in the way of that."

She looked at him sideways and giggled. "Then I suppose we'll just have to run through the jungle spearing him and chasing him and spearing him again until he either gets tired or dies."

Greg looked back at the boar, then at Amanda. "This is a side of you I've never seen."

"Come on! How hard can this be?" She hefted her spear into one hand, testing the weight of it as though she had any idea at all what she was doing. "Let's go."

They stalked the boar, being as quiet as they could, circling widely around him and trying to come up from behind. The thing was so engrossed in his meal that he didn't notice them until it was too late. By the time Amanda and Greg emerged from the bushes, spears at the ready, the boar was quite full, lazy and without care.

Amanda never hesitated, didn't question her abilities or her desire. She drew back that spear and let it fly with all her might. Having never thrown a spear (or much of anything else, for that matter) in her life, she had no idea what she was doing. The spear flew true, wavering little, and biting deep when it landed. The moment of exhilaration that Amanda had felt at throwing the spear dwindled rapidly as she watched it bury itself into the sand some ten feet beyond where the boar stood.

By now, the boar had realized that its life was in peril. Whether or not it had ever encountered humans was anybody's guess, but it certainly had encountered danger. With a loud snort and screech, it drove itself forward, directly toward where Greg now stood, trying to make up his mind about the hunt. Its short legs carried the boar surprisingly well. It ran for the brush at breakneck speed.

Greg turned to chase it, his spear at the ready, while Amanda retrieved her spear from the sand where it stood, looking for all the world like a flag pole without its flag. They were both off then, chasing through the jungle in hot pursuit of the boar as it crashed and stumbled its way through the bushes.

Despite the sometimes-wild, sometimes-careful throwing of spears, the boar ran on and survived to find itself cornered in an outcropping of rocks at the base of the mountain. It had led them on a merry chase, leaving them breathless and weak and more frustrated than angry. Once, the boar tried to make his escape over the lowest part of the rocks, but his short legs were unequal to the task and it tumbled, end over chubby end, back to the ground.

Amanda wondered briefly why the thing didn't just attack them. It had those vicious-looking tusks and sizeable teeth. Not to mention its formidable hooves. But it just stood there, backed into the rocks, chuffing and stamping and staring at them with its beady eyes. Greg and Amanda faced it down, their eyes squinted against the sun, spears clutched in a death-grip.

"Go ahead, it's your boar," Greg said between clenched teeth.

"You have better aim. You're stronger. Go ahead." She glanced at him quickly, unwilling to let the boar out of her sight for more than a second.

"It's your prize. You earned it. Go on." He checked her face, saw what he knew to be true.

She raised the spear, cocked her arm further back, tilted her body a bit. There was much readjusting of the spear, perfection of aim. And finally her arm dropped and she started to cry. "I can't."

When she looked back at him, he was leaning on his spear, smiling. "I know." He laughed then, though not at her but rather at the situation. "Neither can I."

"I guess we'll stick with fish," she laughed, going to his arms, hugging him tightly.

Hand in hand, they turned to leave, their breath only barely having returned. They walked slowly, their legs shaky and their energy sapped from the run. And then they realized that the boar was following them. He moved slowly, stayed some twenty feet back, but he was definitely following them.

"What is it with the animals on this island?" Amanda laughed.

"At least he isn't charging at us."

Amanda spun and fixed the boar with a steely stare. "If only you could lay eggs," she told it.

The day burned brightly and it wasn't long before all evidence of the rainstorm had been erased, dissipated like a bad dream. With the boat done, Greg and Amanda turned their attention to food. The storm had churned up the waters, washing all manner of things onto the beach: jellyfish, driftwood, shells, seaweed and a bucket. It was a plain white bucket, cracked at the top but still of some use.

They used sticks to poke the jellyfish back into the water and took turns working the net in order to catch some crabs. The boat, still more sculpture than usable craft, sat majestically on the sand. The storm seemed not to have touched it at all. Being on the beach meant that they could watch for passing craft. They didn't want to alert the enemy to their presence, but anything short of the Japanese fleet would have been welcome.

They took a break to eat lunch, dining on pineapple and some questionable nuts which turned out to be cashews. They sat in the shade, watching the sky play with the ocean and all of a sudden, Amanda became aware of a shadow beside her. She jumped and squealed, whipping her head around to stare Cheetah straight in the eye.

"There you are!" she laughed, taking his hand and patting it. "Where did you get to during the storm?"

And Cheetah stared at her.

"He must have a safe place of his own," Greg offered. "Surely he wasn't sitting around in a tree during that awful storm."

"Are you hungry, boy?" She put out her hand, offering up a piece of pineapple. Cheetah took it and nibbled at it, his eyes on her the whole time. "I wonder if he's lonely . . . not having any other chimps around."

"That might be why he hangs out with us. We're the closest thing to chimps that he has."

Amanda nodded. A sound reached her ears then; a sort of dull, soft roar coming from high up and somewhere behind her. She stood suddenly, eyes trained on the sky, her hand shading her face. "Do you hear that?"

"Yea." Greg frowned and stood to look for the source of that noise. It grew steadily louder, though he still couldn't pinpoint its source. "It's a plane."

"One of ours?"

"Don't know. I can't see it. God, I wish I had a pair of binoculars."

They continued to search the sky, back to back, squinting against the bright noon-day sun. Then: "Look! There it is!"

The plane was flying low, puttering along almost as though it were looking for something. She couldn't see the markings at first, though she screwed up her face and willed her eyes to zoom in on it. "It's one of ours. Look! See that woman painted on the nose."

They ran then, ran for all they were worth toward the beach, screaming and waving madly. They jumped up and down, hollering and gesturing, praying that someone in that plane would see them.

Greg sighed and let his arms drop as the plane moved out of range. "They can't hear us for the engine noise. And I guess they don't have a spotter . . . or he isn't bothering to look down."

Amanda's spirits fell along with her smile. "You'd think they'd look to see whether the Japanese had set up a base on the island. Something." She felt like crying, her shoulders slumped and she dropped to the sand, hugging her legs. "God, they were so close."

"We don't know that they didn't see us," Greg soothed, sinking down to sit behind her. He wrapped one arm around her shoulders and pulled her close. "They might circle back around."

"They were so close, we almost could have hit them with a rock," she said so softly that he nearly missed it.

"Next time," he said, rubbing her arm. "Now, let's catch a few more crabs and take a swim, hmm?"

She nodded, let him help her up. Just then, she was caught between wanting to throw a tantrum and collapsing on the beach in a fit of tears. One chance. One chance in all that time and they hadn't seen them. The flare gun was all the way back at the cave and the plane wasn't coming back. They had had one shot to escape the island and they had missed it.

CHAPTER EIGHT

The morning stole Amanda's sleep from her and she grumbled as she tried to hide her face in the tangle of muscle that was Greg. He shifted to accommodate her, his own eyes testing the bright light and finding it too strong for his liking. They huddled together for a few moments, their eyes adjusting, their minds at war with their bodies. Sleep was coveted but the demands of their bodies kept it at bay.

"You go first," said Amanda. "It's your turn."

Greg rose at once, stretching and yawning, pulling his pants on slowly and stumbling across the cave. She giggled at him in sympathy and rolled over, stealing his spot on the bed, the one in the shadows.

"Be right back," he yawned, slipping out of the cave and disappearing from her sight.

She sat up, struggling to make sense of her clothes and pull them on. Outside, the clouds were motionless and the palm fronds barely swayed. Already, the heat and humidity had begun to rise. It was a good day for sitting in the cool shade of the pond.

Greg stumbled back through the bushes and into the clearing, his hands full of passion fruit and mangoes. He went to the flat rock to prepare them and she disappeared into the jungle. When she returned, he was on his second mango, his face drenched in juice and his eyes finally open.

"It's going to be high tide in about two hours. The boat will be easiest to move then."

"Okay," she said idly.

"Once we find out if it's seaworthy, then we can see about getting that motor to work."

"Okay," she muttered again.

"Amanda, are you all right?" he asked, watching her face.

"Yeah. I'm fine. I was just thinking about that plane. What's the range for a plane like that?" Her brow was furrowed and lines had begun to appear around her eyes.

"Well, I think it was a D-9, so the range would be about four hundred miles. Why?"

"They had to take off from somewhere, so that means that there's a base or an aircraft carrier somewhere within 400 miles of here."

Greg pulled a face and then smiled. "Actually, it's probably closer. Unless they were on a one-way trip, they wouldn't go any further than their fuel could get them with a return trip."

"So, about two hundred miles. There could be a ship or a base just two hundred miles from here. And they could be headed this way."

"Not that that does us any good unless they come near enough to see us."

She nodded again and bit into a passion fruit. The island was heady with the scent of passion flowers, a perfume more glorious than any laboratory creation. The fruit was just as delicious and she moaned as she bit into it. Cheetah appeared, a banana in his hand. He sat down next to her, bit the end off the banana and spit it out. Then he offered the banana to Amanda. Giggling, she took a bite, gave him a piece of passion fruit, and smiled.

"I need to wash up a bit," Greg said, standing and offering his hand. "Let's go down to the beach. We can watch the tide move in and clean up."

She took his hand and instinctively stuck her other hand out behind her, offering it to Cheetah. The trio made their way through the jungle hand-in-hand, ambling slowly along. It dawned on her then that their rescue would leave Cheetah alone on the island, save for the wild pig which they had seen only once. She wondered if they could take him with them when they left. She wondered if they should.

Greg and Amanda plowed into the surf, stripped of their clothes and, for the moment at least, all cares. They scrubbed up and swam, then found the heat of the water oppressive and climbed out. The tide was rolling in all the while, lapping at the stern of the boat, washing things in and out of the sea. Finally, Greg stood up from the beach and gave his hand to Amanda.

"I think we should give the boat a go, don't you?"

She nodded and let him help her up, smiling at him as she slipped into his arms. "I don't think the tide will get much higher. This is our best chance."

"You take one side and I'll take the other. Lift a little as you push so it doesn't drag on the beach too much."

"You know it's a boat, right?" she laughed, taking her position just shy of the bow.

"It's heavy, I know. But try to lift it as much as you can."

On three, they heaved into it, lifting the boat as much as possible and pushing it toward the water. The aft end was nearly afloat and as they pushed, making painfully slow progress, the stern of the boat became lighter, more buoyant. Red-faced and muscles straining, they lifted and pushed, lifted and pushed, until the bow broke free of its sand prison and came afloat.

"Can you see anything?" Amanda asked from her position on the ocean's bottom. "Is it staying dry?"

"Can't tell," Greg answered, straining to lift his line of sight above the deck. "We should get in and see what's what."

He gave her a leg up, grinning to himself as she hauled herself upward and over the edge of the deck. Then he leaped, off like a shot and onto the deck, slinging one leg over the side and then the other. He sat on the bench, looking at his patchwork repair on the hull.

"It seems dry." He smiled. "By God, I think we did it!"

"Yes!" she hollered, shooting up one hand for a high five.

Greg's face fell, his eyes darkening and looking very confused. "What the hell are you doing?"

She looked at her hand, then at him, lowering her hand with a sigh. "It's called a high five. Whenever something awesome happens, people slap each other's hands and it's called a high five."

"It looks like a Nazi salute." His tone was flat, deep.

"Well, you left me hanging, so of course it does. Try it. Just smack my hand."

"No."

"Come on. Everybody does it where I come from." She watched

him stare at her, his gaze level and his face expressionless. Then she sighed and gave up. "So, now what?"

"Let's give it fifteen minutes or so, just to make sure it's gonna hold. Then we'll haul it back up to the beach and I'll tinker with the motor a bit."

"While you do that, I want to climb our mountain again. Maybe I can see some ships on the horizon or something."

"Promise you'll be careful?" He took her hand then, stroked her fingers gently with his thumb.

"I promise." She offered up a smile, then watched as he kissed her hand.

In silence they waited, feeling the sway of the boat on the waves and staring at the patch, praying that it would stay dry. After fifteen minutes, there wasn't a sign of water anywhere inside the boat, so they slipped back into the water and towed the boat to shore. It took a lot of heaving and pulling but in the end, they beat the sand and the pull of gravity and managed to dry-dock the boat.

She stood on her toes and pecked his cheek. "You did an awesome job of fixing the boat, Greg. Now, you have fun with that motor. I'll go see what I can see from the mountain."

She walked briskly away and had gone no more than twenty feet when Greg called to her. "I love you, Amanda."

She cast a glance back over her shoulder and smiled. "I love you, too, Greg."

She strode away whistling then, headed for the mountain and a clear view of the sea. Cheetah had wandered off somewhere the minute they had begun fussing with the boat, so she went alone, humming and whistling as she walked. The heat was not as bad in the shade of the palms and the going was much easier.

When she began to climb the mountain, however, she was in full sun, the rays beating down on her, drawing sweat from every pore and nearly blinding her with it. She proceeded carefully, not as scared this time but still cautious. No telling what she would see from the top of the mountain now. Visions raced through her head of a huge fleet of American ships, slowly making their way just past the island, their flags flying in the breeze, men parading at quarters. It was a feeble hope. The odds were against her. Still, she couldn't help but play it out in her mind.

An hour later, she was nearly to the top of the mountain. From the corner of her eye, she saw a large bird, possibly a crane, fly across the opposite beach. It was graceful and white and the sun gleamed off its feathers. She wished for all the world that she could fly.

Once at the top, she rested, plopping her butt onto the gravel and letting her aching muscles do nothing for a while. The breeze was much stiffer up there and it cooled the sweat on her body into a second skin. She drew deep breaths, trying to clear her head before she stood on those too-shaky legs.

The view stole her breath. Every bit as beautiful as the first time she'd seen it, it was more familiar now, a drop-dead gorgeous work of art that never stopped changing. She smiled to herself and scanned the horizon, looking for movement, for grays among the blue. There was nothing to see but endless ocean and sky. Even the clouds had abandoned her now. She turned to look in the opposite direction. Greg was there, working on the motor. He had his shirt off and his muscles tensed and relaxed.

She marveled at how much she loved him; how quickly she had come to do so. When they did leave the island, however that happened, would the business of real life and the push of others steal that love, lessen it somehow? She worried that dragging him into the future, into her world, might somehow split them apart, make him resent her for it. She could stay here forever, love him forever. Could he?

She looked one more time, watching for any suspicious motion on the waters that lay before her. Was she able to see for ten miles? For a hundred? She had no idea but in all that space she couldn't spot a single thing of note, save for the bird.

The climb back down to earth took longer, hurt more. Her muscles were well-toned by now but they were not used to the task of climbing mountains. By the time her feet were firmly planted on the sand, she was shaking and sore and exhausted. They would eat clams that night, as she doubted that she had the strength even for fishing.

Cheetah ran out of the jungle and into her arms, almost as though he was scared of something. Perhaps the boar had returned or maybe he was just happy to see her. Either way, she nearly dropped him as he leaped, set him down immediately.

"Sorry, pal. You have to walk today. I'm too pooped to pop."

She giggled and took his proffered hand, led him toward the beach and Greg.

"Did you see anything?" he asked as she approached slowly.

"Just a bird. There's nothing out there as far as I can see." She dropped onto the sand in the shade of the boat, frowned into her knees. "How's it going with the motor?"

"Well, I'm no marine mechanic, but I managed to put some oil on the parts that were dry and I blew the sand and salt out of everything I could. I've got this so far." He pulled steadily and gently on the handle and the line wound out about a foot.

"It's better than nothing. Perhaps if you work gently at it, it will unfreeze over time?" She smiled hopefully up at him, her eyes heavily hooded and sleepy-looking.

"That's what I'm hoping. I rotated the motor by hand a few turns, so I think it's just the pull-start that's stuck. I may have to take it apart." He regarded her tired face and dead expression. "You don't look well. Maybe you should go lie down for a while."

She nodded slowly. "Good idea. I'll be in the cave if you need me." She stood painfully and bussed his cheek, letting her hand linger on his taut bicep. An urge rushed over her; one she didn't have the energy to act on. "Maybe after I've rested a bit you can join me?"

He kissed her again, a lingering embrace. "Count on it," he whispered.

Amanda had been so deeply asleep that even dreams couldn't intrude. She was splayed across the communal bed, arms and legs akimbo, head tossed to the side. Even the long drink of water that she had had before lying down didn't disturb her after nearly two hours. But then a strange noise reached her ears, a quick, metallic coughing sound, followed by two staccato revs. Then a dull and distant roar broke loose, settling into a hum.

She sat bolt upright on the bed, panting from the suddenness of it, eyes wild. Had the war arrived in their corner of the world? Was the plane back? She listened intently, head cocked and even her eyes unmoving. The sound. It was familiar and almost soothing now that she heard it fully. And then it struck her, the source of that sound: it was the boat motor. A smile played with her lips and she stood, her legs complaining at the abuse and her back crying out. Quickly, she went to the mouth of the cave, prepared to climb down. Then, a muscle in her right leg cramped, freezing her with a fast gasp and a clamping shut of her eyes. She sat down, hard and fast, and rubbed the pain from her calf.

By the time she was on her feet again, the noise had stopped. She hoped it was because Greg had shut the motor off and not because the thing had run out of gas or just died. She made her way to that first hand-hold on the long trip down, paused as she heard yet another noise. The bushes rustled, there was the sound of something being kicked through the grass.

When she looked to see what had made the noise, Greg was coming through the jungle toward her. Now rested from her journey and feeling mischievous, she hurried to the bed and lay down on it, pretending to be asleep.

Through slitted lids, she saw him standing in the doorway of the cave, his shadow blotting out the sun for a few beats as he doubtless gazed at her. Then he was on his knees on the bed next to her, kissing her belly, teasing a finger from hip to knee, watching the goose bumps chase his touch.

Dinner was forgotten, delayed in the name of love. They enjoyed each other until darkness fell, only then realizing how long they had been wrapped in each other. It was too late to fish, too dark to gather. They contented themselves to a few purloined fruits and a handful of nuts which had been left from a better meal. Then they fell onto the bed and into sleep, the jungle warm and still as a sleeping baby.

Amanda had no idea how late the hour or why she had been awakened. Something shook her, physically, from a sound sleep, leaving her breathless and listening for the thief of her dreams. It came to her in an earth-shuddering boom which rocked the cave and shook the palm trees outside. She rolled into Greg's arms, kissing his chest and sighing her words across his warm flesh.

"Greg? Did you hear that?"

He shifted a bit, put a protective arm around her. "Just another storm. Go back to sleep." He hadn't bothered to open his eyes, hadn't moved a bit.

She listened again. The sound came regularly, like the footsteps of a giant. It had a rhythm. And with each boom, a bright orange flash of light lit up the sky outside. "It's not a storm. Listen."

He peeled open his eyes with a sigh and listened, his face creasing with worry. "Thunder. That's all. Sleep." He rolled over then, tucking an arm over his head.

She was irritated now. "Greg, no. It's not a storm. Look at those flashes of light."

"Lightning."

"It is not. Look at it. It's orange and it flashes with each boom."

Exasperated beyond comprehension, Greg rolled over and sat up. Boom-flash-boom-flash. "Thunder. Lightning. It's a storm. Please, Amanda . . ."

"I'm telling you, it's not a storm." She stood and walked to the opening of the cave, leaned over so as to peer out beyond the waterfall. The sky was alight with orange, flashing and burning, and the forever-booms had come to overlap. "Something's out there. Come look."

With a growl of frustration, Greg stood and walked to her. No protective arm this time; he was far too irritated for that. He watched for a few moments, his face growing ever more twisted with the stress of it. Then, "I'm going to climb up a bit so I can see over these trees."

"Don't leave me."

"It'll be all right." He bent to kiss her on the forehead, then turned away.

"Be careful."

Seconds stretched into minutes, which stretched into decades as she waited for him to return. All the while, her heart quickened its pace until it was trying to beat its way out of her chest. When he at last stepped down onto the rock outcropping of their cave, she nearly cried out from the relief of seeing him. "What is it?"

"You were right. There's ships out there, fighting." His lower lip was caught in the clamp of his teeth and he was squinting into the darkness.

"Can you tell who they are? Who's winning?" Her heart sped again and she felt a cold sweat break out on her brow.

"It's too dark. And they're pretty far out there. Maybe ten miles."

"Do you think they'll come here? What'll we do, Greg?"

"I don't know anything, honey. I wish I did." He sighed, motionless for so long that Amanda thought he had turned to stone. Then he reached up and removed his dog tags, letting them jangle into his hand. "But we have to be ready."

"Ready? Ready for what?" In the darkness, her eyes were wide but blind, her body shaking but immobile. "Ready for what, Greg?"

He was removing his shirt now, the sequel to his uniform pants and the most telling evidence of all. He tucked the dog tags into the pocket, then added his wallet for good measure. The shirt was folded neatly and placed at the very back of the cave, then covered with a rock. He returned to her, no longer sweet, funny Greg with the careless hair, but officer Greg, all business and brevity.

"If they come here, if they find us, we can't let them know that I'm a pilot, okay? Not one word of planes, pilots, military, officers, nothing. You understand."

She nodded, realized that he couldn't see it, then said, "Yes."

"We are a couple. Dating. We left Hawaii for a day on our boat out there and got caught in a storm and ended up here."

"Where? We don't know where we are. Hawaii could be on the other side of the world."

"I'm going with the greatest probability here." He swallowed loudly enough that she could hear it. "So, we're civilians who got trapped here after our boat got caught in a storm. We don't know anything about planes or the war or anything. I own my own garage in Fairbury, Nebraska, and you work at the library."

"Greg, I'm so scared."

He could hear the tears in her voice and he grabbed her suddenly, clutching her to his chest and stroking her hair. He felt the first trickle of tears as it washed down his chest. He held her more tightly. "Chances are, they'll never even come here. They've got more important things to worry about."

She pulled back, gazed up at where she knew his face to be. "But when the battle is over, what then?"

"Well, that's simple. If the Americans win and they show up, we're saved. If the Japanese—I assume it's the Japanese—win and they show up, we hide. We can stay in the cave. It's hidden behind the waterfall and chances are they'll never see it."

"We can't hide forever. What if they put a base here?" Her mind raced ahead, saw all potential problems, tallied them up.

"You can't worry about things that might never happen, honey."

"Oh, like getting caught in time portals and sent back in time or talking to men from the past or getting shipwrecked?" She laughed then, a near hysterical sound that made him afraid for her.

"Yea, like that. We can't be afraid of everything that might happen. But we can plan for the things that probably will." He kissed her softly, cradling her in his arms and sighing. "Now, there's nothing we can do tonight. We have to wait until morning to get a better look at what's going on out there. Let's lie down and try to get some rest."

"Oh sure." She let him lead her back to their bed but she wasn't going to sleep. No way was she going to sleep with all the noise, the light, the fear. Still stiff and tense, she tried to curl into his arms, failed, and merely lay there, staring at a dark ceiling in a dark cave on a dark island.

"I love you, Frank," he said with a smile, as he drifted in and out of sleep.

CHAPTER NINE

Dawn was only two hours away. Amanda had tried to be still but as the minutes ticked by, the stress ate at her resolve until she found herself tossing and turning, thrashing about on the mat that was their bed. For all of that, Greg seemed peacefully asleep, unmoving. It irritated her that he could sleep in the face of such mortal danger, that he wasn't as completely terrified as she was.

When the light outside was bright enough that it crept into their little chamber, Amanda rose from Greg's side and walked to the cave opening. The booming sounds were slower, but louder. She could no longer see the bright orange flashes of night firing, even though the battle seemed closer. The daylight blotted out all other sources of light.

Greg sat up behind her, wiping sleep from his eyes and yawning. When she turned to look at him, he was smiling. "Do you think it's safe to go out there?"

"They're out at sea, Amanda. But if it will make you feel better, I'll climb up and see if it looks like anybody came ashore."

Her smile was instant and broad. "Please?" she asked of him, nodding.

He sighed that very deep, put-out kind of sigh that told her she was being a pain. "Of course."

She watched him as he struggled to his feet, stepping aside to let him pass. With a peck on the lips and a wink, he climbed to that first handhold. If she leaned out just a bit, she could watch his progress. He had only ten or twelve feet to climb before he could see over the tops of the palm trees. He was up there for several minutes, squinting against the sunlight and shielding his eyes as he stared at the horizon. Then he came back to her, his face unreadable.

"Well?"

"Well . . . they're still out at sea. A bit closer, though. Definitely some Japanese ships. They're fighting our boys. I can't really tell who's winning, but one of the Japanese ships is on fire and taking on water."

"Well, that's good, at least." She brightened a bit. More than anything, she wanted those Japanese ships to be sunk, every last one, and for the Americans to come ashore. "Oh my God!"

"What?" Greg looked momentarily scared but he calmed when he saw the look on her face.

"If we can figure out which battle this is, I can tell you who wins. I know a ton about World War Two. My grandpa and his buddies had so many stories that I was fascinated by it. Did you recognize any of our ships?"

"They don't have names on them. Just numbers."

"What numbers? Tell me any one of them."

"I don't know." He blinked. It hadn't seemed at all important at the time, but now it was evidently crucial.

"Okay, no sweat. Do you think it's safe to go out?"

"Yea, sure. I didn't see any sign that there was anybody here."

"Okay, I'm going to go take care of business. Then I'm going to go have a look from our little perch up there. If I can identify the ships, I can tell what battle it is and who won. And I can tell pretty much where we are."

He gaped at her for a moment, at a loss for anything to say. "Be careful out there," was all he could manage.

She hurried down to the ground, intent on having these nagging mysteries solved. For one thing, the presence of both American and Japanese ships meant that they were in the Pacific. Somewhere. The nervous fit which had taken her a few hours ago seemed all but gone now, in the face of a resolution to their problems. There had still been no sign of whatever strange anomaly had brought her here, but that was of no immediate concern.

Rushing through her ablutions, she made it back to the cave in record time, pausing to tell Greg that it was his turn and then heading up the side of the mountain. She had purpose now, and a clear mission: To find out which battle they were witnessing and to recall its outcome. She had read so many volumes about Naval history in general and World War Two history in particular, listened to so many stories. Surely she had the knowledge that she needed.

The rocks were hot this morning, uncomfortable to hold onto at times, but manageable. She made her way to the top quickly, keeping low and not standing up. On the one-in-a-million chance that someone on one of those ships was looking their way through binoculars, she didn't want to be spotted.

Just now, she wished for a pair of binoculars of her own. The battle was closer now, though the ships were still very small in the distance and their numbers unreadable. She squinted hard and willed herself to see it. Three ships she recognized as light cruisers and two as destroyers, but nothing more was discernible. She fought to remember her history, not just the facts and figures she memorized in high school, but the small details she had learned on her own, from her grandpa and his friends.

As she climbed back down, she cursed herself for not knowing what she needed to know and for not having the foresight to keep simple things like blankets and binoculars on the boat. As she stepped onto the rocks outside their cave, Greg met her, his face expectant and his arms ready to receive her.

"So, what do we know?"

She leaned against the wall of the cave, her face contorted with thought and her eyes on the floor. "I still couldn't read any of the numbers. I know there are three light cruisers and two destroyers. Beyond that, I can't tell anything except that there are no flat-tops out there. I can tell you what it isn't. It can't be the battle of Midway or of the Coral Sea. It's too late for that. It could be the battle of the Leyte Gulf, but I'm not sure of the date. I do know that the Battle of Kula Gulf was in July of 1943, so that's a strong possibility."

"Did we win that one?"

"We did." She sighed, folded her arms over her chest and frowned. "I think we can safely say that we're in the South Pacific . . . somewhere near the Solomon Islands, perhaps. There's a long string of battles in this area, some won and some lost. I could see that the one Japanese ship was already sunk. Men are in the water and they're not making any attempt to save them. They might end up here. One of the light cruisers has been hit on the bow, but I can't tell if she's going down or not. I'm not much help, am I?"

He stroked a finger over her cheek and smiled. "You're more help than you know."

"All I could think when I was standing up there was what would happen if that light thing came back right now. A dozen ships would find themselves smack dab in the middle of 2012 without ever knowing how or why."

He hugged her gently, stroking her back and frowning at the wall of the cave behind her. "I guess we should go down to the beach. We can grab a few fish, have a last good meal. Then I think we should keep to the cave as much as possible until this is all over with."

"I think you're right. I just wish we had one single usable weapon between us."

Greg smiled and pulled away, reaching to the wall and grabbing one of the spears which had been leaning there. "Not a problem. We have these nifty, handy-dandy spears. We can just poke a bunch of holes in 'em 'till they leak like sieves." He made a parody of a fight, lashing out with the spear and dancing around. It made her laugh and that's all he was going for.

"Let's go eat fish." She smiled and held out her hand.

Hand in hand, they walked down to the beach. He caught the fish, she dug up clams for steaming. There was a kind of serenity in the knowledge that, whatever happened, a resolution was close at hand. Besides, at her current level of stress, Amanda would have had a stroke long before the Japanese ever got to her.

They watched the battle as they prepared the fire and cooked the fish. Another American ship was hit and the first had gone down. Unlike the Japanese, the American ships were taking on men from those wounded and dead ships and it was the cause of their downfall.

By dusk, it became clear that the Americans held little hope of winning the day. The air was filled with smoke and the prevailing winds pushed it to the island, smelling of fuel and explosives. The first light cruiser had gone down without notice, but as each subsequent ship was hit and began to sink, Japanese and American alike, the sounds of metal folding in on itself and twisting out of proportion was heard all the way to the island.

Greg and Amanda watched it all, tears in their eyes, from the shade of a palm tree. They were less visible there, cooler and more comfortable. The last two remaining American ships turned tail and chuffed away, the remainder of the Japanese fleet hot in their wake. Amanda felt her heart sink, her head pound with the knowledge that they would not be rescued today. The water was filled with bodies, both alive and dead, some clinging to bits of debris and trying to stay afloat.

"We can't do anything," she whispered. "We can't risk changing it."

Beside her, Greg nodded agreement and took her hand. "We should go to the cave. If any of them make it to the island . . ."

"I know," she spat, stopping him before he could say the one thing that scared her most.

In silence, they picked their way through the half-lit jungle. She had seen no sign of the boar or Cheetah in two days. She hoped they were hiding, safe. Her mind raced all the way back to stories she had heard of Japanese soldiers being stranded on tropical islands, never aware that the war had ended, even some twenty years later. She wondered if the men who now fought for their lives in the ocean would become some of those storied soldiers.

". . . grab some fruit as we go. We might be in there for a while."

She puzzled over what Greg had been saying as she was lost in her thoughts. Something about fruit. She snapped out one hand and grabbed a mango, then another. Papayas were purloined as she walked, filling her head with more frightening thoughts and her arms with fruit.

"Will anyone come back for the sailors who were lost?" she asked reverently.

"The Japanese never do. I'm not sure about the Americans. The South Pacific is a hotbed of battles. They might wait until the war is over."

"Two years," she sighed morosely. "The war ends in 1945. But I didn't just tell you that."

He regarded her briefly, from the corner of his eye. "We win?"

"Mmm-hmm," she said with a quick nod. "So we'll hide in the cave until someone friendly comes along and then we can be rescued. What if that thing comes back in the meantime?"

"Then we have to find a way to get to the boat and off the island in time to meet it. At all costs."

Again she nodded. "I'm going to climb up one last time, just to see what's going on around our island."

He kissed her forehead, her nose, bussed her lips. "I love you, Amanda. More than I've ever loved anyone or anything in my whole life."

"I love you too, Greg." She spared one quick, hard hug for him and then started up the side of the mountain once more.

"What will they do to us if they catch us?" she asked. She had climbed the mountain and seen things that she wished she would never see again. The water on their beach side was peppered with bodies and debris. The debris had begun to float ashore and she cursed herself for having been happy about that; thinking first of what they might glean from the sailors' misfortune. In the opposite direction, she had seen a small fleet of ships headed for the island. They were clearly Japanese, clearly not geared for heavy fighting. In fact, she had first thought them to be PT Boats, but realized all too quickly that they were too large for PT Boats.

"It depends." Greg was sullen and quiet. She knew that all of this had hit him harder. It was his time, these were his people. He might know some of the men who now bobbed in the water.

"On what?" She watched his face, frowning.

"On the nature of the men who capture us. On whether or not they believe our story. If they think we're civilians, they might just hold us in a prisoner of war camp until the end of the war. Or they might just leave us here. But if the man in charge is a vicious man, he might just have us killed so that he can brag of the two Americans he slaughtered. Or he might not believe us and he might torture us or . . ."

"I'm sorry I asked."

"Whatever happens, just do everything they say. Don't resist. A woman has a better chance of survival than a man. It's considered weak to kill a woman."

Tears tracked down her cheeks and fell from her chin. "I don't care, because if they kill you, I don't want to live."

He grabbed her chin in his hand, forced her eyes to meet his. It was a frightening, sudden gesture and it drew a gasp from her parted lips. "Yes, you do. No matter what happens to me, you go on living. If we get separated, I will find you. I will always find you."

He crushed her lips to his, feeling her tremble, locking his arm around her and pulling her tightly against his chest. She was sobbing, her whole body shaking with the effort of it, but she responded to his embrace. There was desperation in her as she clutched at his back, pulling herself to him as though she could simply melt into him.

Slowly, he lowered them to the bed, his hand cupping the back of her head, setting it gently upon the mat. And then he was on top of her, his mouth devouring hers, hips almost but not quite crushing her as he prepared to make love to her one final time. And still she clutched at him, as if the simple act of making love to him would grant her absolution.

Amanda awoke to a hand clamped over her mouth. She screamed soundlessly against it and began to thrash and struggle against the other hand which held her arm.

"Don't make a sound," said the voice in her ear.

More voices reached her then, multiple voices outside and down below. Reality finally came to her and she nodded against the hand that held her mouth. It was released at once and she drew the first big gulp of air that she'd had in what seemed like hours.

Lips brushed against her ear as Greg whispered softly. "Grab the mat and get back against the wall. Way back in the back and hunker down. Don't make a single sound. No matter what happens. Promise."

"Promise," she breathed.

She rose silently, grabbing the mat and moving toward the back of the cave, making sure not to drag the mat or trip over anything that would make a noise. Greg had gone the opposite direction but she didn't notice this until she reached the back wall of the cave and turned. She felt her heart skip a beat when she saw him flattered against the wall at the mouth of the cave. Quickly, she put the mats down and hunkered to the floor like he had told her to. Oh, God, she was scared!

She was sure that they would hear the pounding of her heart, echoing through the cave and amplified by the water. Greg was at one with the wall then, as the voices hollered below them. They were clearly Japanese. Perhaps those ships had come looking for their lost sailors after all. Perhaps the sailors had merely reached the island. Either way, it was bad.

The voices came nearer, got louder. And then they went away, got softer. Amanda huddled against the wall, quivering in terror at what might happen next. The cave, which had always seemed so warm and welcoming, now felt cold and resentful of her presence. She stayed there for God knew how long, waiting for Greg to come get her, give her some sign that they were in the clear.

Finally, she felt a hand on her shoulder and she nearly screamed before she could get her hands over her mouth. It was only Greg, she told herself. All was well. Slowly, she stood to full height, feeling the strain on her knees relieved and her back stretching out. He held her then, so gentle that he might have been holding a baby. And only moments before, he had been poised to kill whoever came stepped through the opening.

"Are they gone?" she whispered to him.

"I think so. But they might come back. We have to keep listening."

"What if they're stuck here, like we are? We might never be safe."

"We'll deal with that when it does or doesn't happen. Come on, now. Let's set out these mats and lay down right here."

She couldn't imagine sleeping for the rest of her life, honestly. But the stress had put a terrible strain on her body and had sapped her strength. She lay down on the mat, pressed tightly against Greg and shivering a bit. Within fifteen minutes she was sound asleep.

There was no telling how long after that the voices returned. Amanda was the first to notice them this time, rolling at once into a sitting position, hovering over Greg. "Wake up," she whispered ever so softly. "They're back."

He was awake at once. No hesitation, no wondering. He went straight from sleep to soldier mode, hurrying to the doorway and pressing himself to the wall. The voices were again clearly Japanese, undeniably close. But this time, there were flashlight beams accompanying those voices. One of them played over the waterfall from below. Greg held his breath.

Amanda huddled against that back wall, tried to become one with it. She was shaking again and although she knew she had to be brave and stay quiet, all she wanted to do was scream. She wanted to scream and alert the soldiers below, get it over with and stop the wondering and waiting. Her legs ached still and her breathing was ragged. She made sure to breathe through her nose instead of her mouth, trying to keep quiet.

One voice among all the others grew closer and she cursed herself for not learning Japanese. It was obvious from the directionality of it that he had seen the cave and was climbing up to them. The flashlight beam reappeared, played against the wall of the cave. Then she saw his boots and a scream was so close to freedom that she nearly choked on it.

Amanda drew in a long, slow breath and held it, willing her body to be still, to shrink, to do anything that would prevent them from seeing her. Greg was more than able to handle one Japanese soldier, she told herself. This is what he had trained for.

No, her worried half argued. He had trained to fly a plane, not to kill people in hand-to-hand combat. Still, he had sworn to protect her. She had faith in him.

The flashlight beam struck her eyes and moved on. Its owner was fully in the entrance now, looking the cave over. In the cast-off glow of that weak beam, she saw Greg, his arms taut, his left leg bracing for an attack. She bit into her lip, wanted to close her eyes but couldn't make herself do it. And then the flashlight beam fell on Greg, the soldier taking a step back, opening his mouth. He was going to yell for help, draw a weapon, something.

Amanda felt cold panic rise up in her heart. It froze her muscles and stole her voice and for a moment she thought she might faint dead away.

And then Greg attacked.

CHAPTER TEN

The flashlight flew from the Japanese soldier's hand as he went for his weapon. It lay on the floor, casting a thin beam against the wall and turning the two men into shadows. Greg had shoved off from the wall, leading with his fist and punching the man squarely in the jaw. Stunned, he staggered back only for a step before his hand went for the weapon in the holster at his hip. Greg did not hesitate. He had the man by the head before he could retreat, dragging him down head-first against his chest and twisting hard. The soldier's neck snapped with an audible, sickening sound. The gun fell from the man's hand and he fell from Greg's grasp.

Hysteria welled up in Amanda. She had just seen her sweet, gentle Greg kill a man in under a minute. She knew it had to be done; knew that he was protecting her. But it was brutal and cavalier. Amanda thought she might throw up.

Greg wasted no time. He snatched up the weapon and shoved it into the back of his pants, then dragged the soldier to the back of the cave, depositing him in the corner opposite from Amanda.

Her mind raced. The others had surely seen the soldier climb up to the cave. Eventually, they would become worried and come looking for him. If they came one at a time, everything would be fine . . . probably. But if several came at once, they were doomed. True, they had a gun now, but firing that gun would alert anyone near enough to hear it and they, in turn, would come running to the aid of their fellow soldiers.

In the end, the only thing that really mattered to Amanda was that she and Greg walk out of there alive. If Greg were killed, she would be left at the mercy of those soldiers, subjected to all manner of despicable things. No matter what he had said, she stood up and grabbed the largest rock she could lift, carrying it to the doorway and standing ready. Greg motioned her to go back to the corner but she shook her head and mouthed, "No."

Much discussion went on down below and eventually, someone began calling the soldier's name. Funny how some things remained the same, no matter what language was used. The tone of someone's voice, calling for another, was one of those things. The increasing panic, the desperation. Finally, that steadily-growing-nearer sound as they searched.

Amanda raised the rock over her head, waiting, arms trembling and breath coming in big gulps. Another flashlight beam lit the cave. Another soldier followed it into the cavernous room. Human nature dictated that the man's eyes go first to the dropped flashlight, then to his comrade on the ground. It took perhaps two seconds for him to know the whole story and by that time, Amanda's arms were swinging the rock downward at him as hard as they could.

In that moment of fear and stunned panic, the soldier managed to scream two words. Amanda knew nothing but a few words in Japanese, but she knew that those two words would bring the others scrambling up at them. As the man's knees crumpled, she set the rock down, still shaking from fear.

Greg was standing over the soldier by the time she looked up. He was holding one of the spears, his face a study in blue murder. He brought the spear down, stabbing into the soldier's heart in one quick movement, like Van Helsing going after Dracula. Amanda averted her eyes. She just couldn't watch.

The soldier was stripped of his weapon and extra clips, then tossed into the back of the cave with his buddy. Amanda felt so extremely unwell at that point, that she feared she would throw up and pass out.

They had two guns now, that much was good. But they couldn't hold the soldiers off forever and they couldn't stay hidden in the cave forever. Thanks to the waterfall, fresh drinking water wasn't a problem. But they had enough food for a day, no more. Not to mention the fact that they were now trapped in the cave with two dead bodies and in the tropical heat . . . Amanda didn't want to think about that.

The voices outside had become more excited and though Greg

and Amanda couldn't understand the words, the meaning behind them was not lost. Sunrise was still an hour away and the darkness had crippled Greg and Amanda. They took up their positions by the entrance to the cave. The guns were to be a last-resort weapon, since they wanted to avoid escalation. Greg signaled Amanda to put her gun into the waistband of her jeans, then readied himself for the next assault.

The next soldier through the door already had his weapon drawn and ready. Amanda cocked her arms back, ready to unleash the rock on his head, but Greg beat her to it. A quick right cross staggered the man backward, giving Amanda a clear shot at his head. The next soldier was coming through the doorway and he had company.

A shot rang out, echoing in the cave until Amanda's ears began to ring. She was too late in the swing to stop the rock by then and it collided with the soldier's head, driving it against the wall and dropping him to the ground. She was panting, frantic, near the breaking point. Barely had she recovered from that mighty swing when two more men appeared in the doorway. Greg grappled with the first soldier, gun held high in the air between them. The two soldiers coming through the entrance now both had their guns drawn. The first fired at Greg, but he managed to twist the soldier around, placing him between the bullet and its target. The soldier collapsed into Greg's arms and slid slowly to the ground. Even after that, Greg was reaching for his gun, prepared to take out the two newcomers.

Amanda wasn't meant for it. As soon as the shot left the soldier's barrel, meant for Greg, she grabbed the man's arm, pulling the gun upward and away from its intended target. She struggled with all her might, trying to work the man toward the entrance, to push him over the edge. Then the barrel of a third gun kissed her temple and she froze. She was panting so hard she feared she might pass out, shaking so hard that her knees knocked. Her hands loosed their grip on the man's arm and shot into the air.

"Please don't hurt us," she begged. "Please."

Words were exchanged in Japanese but Amanda had no idea what was being said. Her eyes darted around the cave, finding the blood, the two bodies at the back, finally Greg's eyes. She began to cry.

Her fear was broken, along with her concentration, when the soldier in front of her pulled her toward the entrance of the cave. He shoved her toward the edge, pointing down toward the other soldiers. Eyes wide, limbs shaking, she began to climb down. She had no idea what to do, what would happen to them. She prayed that they would bring Greg out, so that she could at least see he was all right.

Once she had reached the ground, the man at her back gave her a huge shove, throwing her forward. She scarcely had time to catch the rising ground with her hands, saving her face a scarring collision. They babbled to each other then, milling around and waving their weapons.

Amanda risked a glance upward at the cave. One soldier was on his way down. The other must still be in the cave with Greg. Poor Greg. He had fought so hard to protect her, risking his own life. She prayed that they would spare him, that she would see him again.

His boots appeared at that moment, drawing a small cry from her throat. She sank back on her haunches as a wave of nausea and dizziness struck her. As Greg reached the ground, the soldier waiting for him grabbed his hands, yanking them viciously behind his back and securing them with a length of rope. Amanda stayed where she was, watching in silence. Apparently, they didn't consider her a threat, for they neglected to bind her hands.

She was yanked to her feet then, her gaze finally able to meet Greg's. He tried to smile for her but his face was unequal to the task. Already, his jaw had begun to swell and his eye turned toward purple. It made Amanda want to cry.

They were shoved together, yelled at in Japanese. There were four guns on them now, none at their disposal. Amanda looped her hand through Greg's bound arm, leaned her face into his arm, and began to cry. A gun poked her in the back then and she stumbled forward. They were being marched to some unknown destination. Apparently, they had not found Greg's things; they didn't know he was a pilot. That much was in their favor at least.

They walked to the beach, urged forward by the occasion poke of a gun into their backs. Their arms were still linked and Amanda still sobbed. Greg's arm was soaked with her tears. As the jungle spit them out, they finally laid eyes on their destination. A Japanese landing ship waited for them. It stood alone just off the coast. Battered and beginning to rust, the craft was broad in the beam and low to the water. Obviously, it was meant to hold troops and gear, a fact that the cavernous interior bore out.

Amanda took a quick check of the beach, saw her boat exactly where they had left it. It didn't appear to have been touched and her heart skipped a beat as she realized that she was about to be separated from it. If the time anomaly required her to be in the same boat when she passed back through it, she was done for.

A smaller, inflatable boat waited for them on the sand. It was larger than a life raft, capable of holding twelve soldiers in complete comfort. She was shoved forward again, the soldier in charge pointing at the raft and pulling her arm from Greg's. Her eyes found his and locked there, brimming with tears. He nodded once and she moved forward, stepping carefully to the boat and sitting when told to. With the frail woman in place, they pushed the boat into the water, then boarded it carefully. Greg was hauled up into the boat, shoved to the back and yelled at to sit.

Once more, Amanda buried her face in his arm, trying to cry but lacking the tears to do it. She would have given anything if he could have put his arms around her then. Anything.

"Do what they say. Cooperate." He nodded as he spoke, then risked a kiss on her cheek. "I'm sorry."

"For what?" she asked, stricken.

"For breaking my promise and not keeping you safe."

The tears came then, flowing over her lids and down her cheeks in rivulets. "You didn't fail me. You didn't."

It was a short ride to the ship and they spent the time in silence. Amanda kept a tight hold on Greg's arm, pressing toward him, desperate not to be separated from him. The waves tossed the little raft around a bit, just enough to make them all a little uncomfortable.

They tied off to the ship near a gangway, a long staircase affair that led from the water to the deck. From there, they were marched to a room that Amanda assumed must have been a ward room or something similar. It was small and square and bereft of all furniture save for a chair and a small table with a water pitcher and glass on it. They placed Greg in the chair then and pointed to the back corner of the room, indicating that Amanda should sit on the floor. She lowered her head and followed orders, swiping away tears as she went.

The hatch was slammed and locked, leaving the two of them alone in the room. She had never been on a Japanese ship before, but she had watched enough detective shows to know that someone was listening in. Like a lost puppy, she crawled across the floor to sit at Greg's feet, wrapping one arm around his leg and looking up into his ruined face.

"Should I untie you?" she asked softly.

"No. They're watching." He jerked his head toward the side wall and sighed.

Only then did she notice the small window on the side wall. She had taken it to be a mirror or a picture of some sort but apparently it was a two-way mirror. She nodded her understand and laid her head on his leg. "What are we going to do?"

"I'm more interested in what they're going to do. I guess we're lucky they didn't kill us right off the bat." He leaned down and pretended to kiss her head, whispering. "They can hear us. Be careful."

She nodded again. "I love you, Greg. I'm sorry our little vacation turned out to be such a mess."

"It's my fault for not checking the weather." He offered a smile that felt genuine, made his jaw hurt. "I love you, too."

The hatch opened then and a fresh face stepped inside. From the medals on his chest and the hat he wore, Amanda guessed that he was an officer. He smiled at them as he paced slowly toward the chair, his hands behind his back and his eyes on Amanda. She felt herself tremble, felt the sting of fresh tears.

"Welcome aboard my ship." He bowed slightly and smiled. His English was flawless. "Might I ask your name, please?"

He was looking directly at Amanda and she cleared her throat before speaking. "Amanda." She felt his eyes roam over her, blushed at the realization.

"Amanda. Very good." He straightened, looking pleased with himself for some reason. "Amanda, would you be so kind as to sit in the corner, please. I do not want any blood to get on you."

She gasped then, her eyes wide and her jaw drooping. When

finally she found her voice, it was deep and husky, laced with fear. "Oh, please don't hurt him. Please. He was just trying to protect me. Your soldiers gave him no choice . . ."

"Amanda, I am not concerned with the deaths of those men. Men die all the time. They were proud to do so. What I want to know is why you and your man were all alone on an uninhabited island."

"It was my fault," Greg volunteered with a touch of humor in his voice. "I failed to check the weather reports. You saw our little boat there? We got caught in the storm several nights ago and the boat was smashed against the rocks around the island."

"You do know that we're in the middle of a war, yes?" He cocked his mouth to one side in a crude parody of a smile.

"We never claimed we were smart." Greg laughed a bit. The sound echoed against the heavy metal walls.

"Madam, please, I ask you again to move back into the corner."

His voice was low and measured but she looked into his eyes and saw anger brewing. She moved at once to the corner, not wishing to ignite a fury which he would take out on Greg. The metal walls were cool to the touch and totally alien to her. She shuddered deep inside and felt tears choke off her air.

"So, you two go off on a holiday in the middle of the greatest war this world has ever known. I see. Why would anyone do such a thing?" He paced as he spoke, his steps timed to match his words, his words slow and precise.

Greg looked up at him, offering a direct—and hopefully guileless—stare. "Do you have a wife, sir?"

"I do." There was a quick smile as he remembered something, possibly his own wife.

"Then you know how insistent a woman can be. And how it's much easier to do what she asks rather than resist her and end up doing it anyway."

The officer seemed to give this some thought, his head suddenly pivoting to bring his eyes to bear on Greg. He laughed. "Indeed I do, sir. What is your name, please?"

"Greg."

"Greg. So then, Greg, you and your wife . . ."

". . . Girlfriend . . ." Amanda corrected.

"Ah, I see. Girlfriend. Is there also a wife then?" His tone was mocking, accusatory. It had become like nails on a chalkboard to Amanda.

"No. Amanda and I have been seeing each other for a while. But we're not married."

"Yes, yes. So, I see. You and your girlfriend take off for holiday, in a small boat. And you are caught in a storm and stranded on a small island. Am I right?"

"That's the crux of it, yes." Greg watched the man. He had stopped pacing and that fact made Greg twitchy.

"You, sir, are very stupid. Surely you do not expect me to believe you? You killed two Japanese soldiers with your bare hands and nearly killed two more."

"When you grow up on a farm with four mean older brothers, you learn a thing or two about fighting."

Amanda watched the exchange from her corner, frightened that the man had found them out, that he had picked up on some tiny detail they had forgotten. She licked her lips and caught her lower lip in the vice of her teeth.

"You fight like a soldier . . . Greg." He spat the name out like a particularly spoiled piece of meat. "And that is what I believe you to be." He leaned down, put his face directly in front of Greg's and stared at him. "But no matter," he laughed, standing up suddenly and beginning to pace once more. "I can prove nothing, so maybe you tell me the true story. Maybe you do not."

Thinking that anything she might say at that point would either give them away directly, or caused the man to suspect their lies, Amanda kept her tongue.

"So, my little ship is on its way to Palawan now," he began, still pacing steadily. "We will pick up more troops there and it is there where we shall part ways."

"What's in Palawan?" Amanda asked at last, her curiosity and worry getting the better of her.

"My dear Amanda, Palawan is home to the Puerto Princesa Prison Camp. It will be your new home." His eyes glinted at that last, making a chill run up Amanda's spine.

"Oh, please no!" she cried, her eyes huge and pleading. "Please, oh please, can't you just let us go? We're no threat to you. We just want to go home."

His face went dark then, the severe angle of his jaw made more pronounced as he clenched it tightly. "I have not killed you. That is mercy enough." Then he spun on his heel and marched away.

Amanda waited for the sound of the lock engaging before she crawled to Greg. She was crying again, pitifully, and her face was in ruin. "What are we going to do?" she asked softly, her head dropping to his knee, her body wracked with sobs.

He leaned down to press a gentle kiss to her cheek and whispered, "Wait."

CHAPTER ELEVEN

It wasn't long before the commanding officer sent back another man to untie and move them. He spoke not a word, merely pointed in the direction he wished them to go. His manner was neither tolerant nor threatening and Amanda guessed that he harbored at least a little ill will toward them for killing his shipmates. He was not as churlish as the others had been, however, partly owing to the fact that he was so much smaller than the others.

They were moved to an actual cell deeper in the belly of the ship. The walls were solid with no windows of any kind and the one door was metal with a small grated opening part way up. It was colder in there, and darker. A single twin mattress lay on the floor but there was a blanket, that much was in their favor. A lone bulb lit their cell from the outside, casting a small square of light through the grate in the door.

Amanda rubbed her arms to ward off the chill, watching as the sailor and his assistant carried in two plates of food and a pitcher of water. He disappeared into the hallway for a moment, leaving his assistant to guard the prisoners. When he returned, he carried a large metal bucket. They were sealed in then, cut off from the world, from light. Amanda felt tears sting her eyes again.

"We have to assume we're still being listened to," Greg said softly, taking her in his arms and holding her. "Be careful what you say."

"All right." She sank into his warmth, eyes closing. Only then did she realize how very exhausted she was. "What are we going to do?"

"I'm not sure yet. But we have to be careful, whatever we do."

She nodded and sighed, her hopes of ever getting back home

dwindling with each passing moment. "We should eat though. It's been a long time."

She took up the plates and moved to sit on the floor. There was rice and what looked like fish balls on the plate; no silverware of any kind had been brought. She watched as Greg sat down next to her, then handed him a plate. In silence they ate, slowly and with great relish. The food was well-prepared and still warm. All in all, it wasn't bad. Amanda thought of the many fish fries, sitting by the fire and cooking fish wrapped in banana leaves, dining on crabs and steamed clams. It made her smile. Funny that those seemed to be the good ol' days.

When they had finished, Amanda put their plates by the door and returned to Greg's side. "I wish we were back on the island," she murmured, feeling him shift to place his arm around her.

"So do I," he agreed. "Whoever thought . . ."

"Yea," she said, cutting him off before he could say something that would bring more tears.

For a few moments, they sat in silence, holding each other and lost in their own thoughts. The small cell smelled of rust and mildew; the mattress smelled of sweat. In the end, exhaustion won out and Amanda crawled to the mattress to lie down. Her head throbbed and her body ached. She knew it was from stress, but it felt like she had run a marathon or spent two hours lifting weights. Sleep stole her quickly and the last realization she had was that Greg was lying next to her and somehow—somehow—it was going to be all right.

She awoke to the sound of the door being opened once more, the keys jangling against the metal of the door and grinding in the old lock. She sat up quickly, only then realizing that Greg was still at her side. She had dreamed while she was asleep. But this horrible situation was no nightmare, as she'd hoped. Two more plates were slid across the floor to them, the door shut and relocked. Amanda retrieved the plates for them and sat cross-legged on the mattress to eat.

"How long was I out?" she asked in wonderment. Her eyes felt puffy and she was grateful for the dim light so that Greg couldn't see how worn and haggard she must look.

"I don't know. I was asleep too. Maybe a couple of hours." He pushed a fish ball into his mouth and groaned.

"If we're in here, we have no idea what's happening out there, if you catch my drift." She meant the anomaly. The thing could pass right by the little ship and they would never know it.

"I know. And I'm not sure what we could do if we saw it." There was a moment of silence while he ate and thought things over. "I wish I could see the rest of the ship. I wish I had some idea how many men are on it."

"And where in the world we are." The sound of metal plate sliding against metal floor broke the pristine silence. She settled back against the wall.

"Come lie down with me," Greg said, tugging at her arm. She slipped down onto the small mattress, settling in against him. He put his arm around her, pulled her close. His lips brushed her ear. "If we have a chance to go topside," he whispered, ever so quietly, "we could go over the side . . . if we see the thing, that is."

She nodded agreement, idly stroking his arm. "I'm a strong swimmer. I could make it."

"It's decided then. If we're up there and we see it, you go over the side and swim as fast as you can toward it. I'll hold them back, keep them from shooting you."

"No," she barked, louder than she intended. "I'm not leaving you behind. We go together or we don't go at all."

"It's the only way," he said, hugging her more tightly. Even in that wretched place, smelling of foul things and filled with the noise of machinery, he wanted her.

"I won't do it. I won't leave you."

He kissed her then, hard and long, letting his breath wash over her cheek and his hands clutch at her in desperation. "I love you, Amanda. I want you to live. I can survive anything if I know you're back home, safe, away from harm."

"And I won't survive a day if I have to go home without you. Now shut up and kiss me again."

Night must have come, for the noises of the ship quieted, the echoing footsteps became scarce. Only the steady roar and deep hum of the engines remained. No more food was brought and, though they couldn't tell exactly when morning had arrived, food was brought shortly after activity on the ship increased. There was no fish with the rice this time; there was some sort of fruit instead.

It was tasty and refreshing and Amanda found that she was oddly grateful for whatever they brought her.

No sooner had they finished their morning meal when the door opened again, the same attending sailor peering in at them. He rattled off something in Japanese and waved frantically at them. They stood and headed for the hall, where another man waited. Together, the four walked up the steps to the deck, where the commanding officer was waiting, his face freshly shaved and a smile firmly in place.

"Good morning, Amanda and Greg." His hands were behind his back, though he didn't pace. His back was board-straight and his eyes bright. "The Geneva Convention requires that I give you two hours of sunlight and exercise per day. As your host, I, Commander Mitsu, have obeyed the Geneva Convention."

"Thank you," Amanda said, offering up what she hoped would be a sincere smile.

"I trust you will not try to escape, please. The sharks in these waters are quite hungry. They will eat you before you can reach shore. Or you will be shot. Enjoy your day."

He spun on one well-shined heel and marched off, closing the hatch after him and locking it. Amanda checked Greg's expression but he was already surveying the area. Whatever the reason, whatever the outcome, it was nice to see sunshine and breathe fresh air again.

"He's probably right about the sharks," Greg mentioned. He was on the move, looking over the side, peering at every hatch and protuberance on the deck. "But if we got close enough to a shore line, I'd be willing to risk it. Damn," he said to himself as much as to her. "No life boats."

Amanda came to stand next to him, shoulders touching as she leaned in to whisper. "Perhaps if we had some sort of weapon against the sharks. A sharp piece of metal or knife, something."

"It would help." He paced the perimeter of the deck, looking over the side, frowning. "I've been watching faces. This ship has lost a lot of men. None of the landing vehicles or equipment are in the cargo bay. I don't see a lot of different men on the ship. I think they've lost a battle recently."

She nodded and wrinkled her nose. "From the smell of things

down there, they're taking quite a few back for burial."

"I don't know about that." He began to meander slowly along the starboard side, making his way toward the pilot house at a slow pace, trying to maintain a casual demeanor. "But I do know that there can't be any more than twenty men on this boat."

She watched him cruise the pilot house, looking from the corner of his eye so as not to draw attention. She followed him for part of it, then finally came to rest against a gun turret near the port bow. When he came back around to where she was leaning, he had a smile on his face. "I've got it," he whispered, leaning in, then pecking her cheek.

Her eyebrows shot up, she grinned a bit. "You know how?"

"I do." He hugged her, let his lips brush her cheek as he whispered. "We're going to take the whole damn boat."

Her head jerked back and she frowned then, her eyes stricken. It took a good deal of fortitude to regain her composure but when she did, she smiled. "You're crazy."

"Like a fox." And he winked.

Days passed and a rhythm was established. Two meals, then an outing to the deck, then one more meal, a change of their water pitcher, and they went to sleep. They knew they were being watched; every word was being listened to. Sometimes, Commander Mitsu joined them on deck. Mostly, they were left to themselves. They had not put up a fuss, had not argued or tried to escape. The way Greg had it figured, their keepers considered them fairly harmless.

After three days of travel, the boat passed into the gulf. There was land to each side of them, so close that they could see people moving about, fishing, washing themselves. It was a primitive-seeming place, but it seemed feasible that they could swim to either side, hold their breath, and manage to surface beyond the range of the Japanese weapons. It was a risk that Amanda thought worth taking.

"It can't be more than three hundred yards to land," she whispered into his ear. They were leaning on the rail, shoulders together, heads tilted in. "We could be out of range before anyone got here with a weapon."

"Can you hold your breath that long?" He checked her face,

weighed her desperation against her honesty.

"Absolutely." She didn't so much as blink. "There's no time. No one is here."

"We'll have to be quick. Jump off hard and fast." He doubted her truthfulness, even with herself. If they got away, the Japanese might give chase. "No looking back. Just swim like hell."

"Right onto the beach."

"They could catch us, come after us in a boat."

"It might be our only shot." She checked his eyes, pleaded with her own. "We have to try."

"But if they kill you . . ."

She stood on her toes and kissed him, a long and lingering embrace that still made her shiver and moan. "Let's do it. Right now."

He took her hand and turned a bit, checking for anyone who might be near them. The deck was empty, the pilot house was manned by only two men and they appeared to be engrossed in their duties. Japanese ships had no safety lines on the deck, so the way to the water was unhindered. Greg placed one hand on the edge of the deck, Amanda following suit. "Go," he said softly.

And they leaped. Releasing each other's hand, they leaped as hard and far as they possibly could. A giant intake of air, an exhalation, another huge gulp of air held and they were on their way. Amanda had been right. It took a full twenty seconds for the man in the pilot house to realize they were gone. And when he did realize it, he still was not sure which direction they had gone.

Amanda cut through the water with her hands, breath held, heart pumping like a hammer in her chest. Her legs kicked and, though she could see Greg in front of her—he having made the longest initial leap—she was not far behind him. After a hundred feet, her breath was still not an issue. She had heard no gunshots, saw no bullets penetrate the water. In her mind, they were very nearly safe.

The water would slow the bullets, lessen their impact. But it would not keep them from being shot. Amanda knew that as well as Greg. So she kept swimming, as fast and as hard as she could. Her lungs wanted air now. They were about 200 feet from the boat and no more than a hundred feet from shore. A few more strokes and her need for air overrode her need to not get shot. She surfaced for a great gulp of air, then dove beneath the surface again. In that one quick instant, she heard the chaos from the boat, the hollering and rushing about. Whatever they were doing back there, they were frantic to get it done. Then came the bullets, slicing cleanly through the water. She saw the little splashes made as the bullets entered the water in front of her and she swam deeper, faster, putting the bullets behind her. But the boat motored on, taking them away from the island.

Finally, the ocean floor rose to meet them and Amanda stood. She couldn't stop her forward momentum, however, and as soon as her feet were under her, she began running. The water pulled at her legs and her wet clothes weighed her down, but she kept going. Greg was there, legs propelling him forward even as he looked back to see where she was.

Once they were on dry land, the people on the beach began to panic. They knew full well that Greg and Amanda were Americans—or at least not Japanese—and that they had jumped off the Japanese landing boat. The good citizens backed away as they came ashore, standing aside and watching benignly as they ran off. They wanted no part of whatever was going on on their beach.

There was no stopping. They had to get out of sight before the Japanese decided to put a boat in the water and come after them. Greg tugged at Amanda's hand, pulling her forward, beginning to run again.

"Come on! We have to hide!" He was panting hard from the exertion, his face red and his muscles still taut and deeply etched from their battle with the surf.

"Yes, yes! Run!" She was gulping air, her teeth chattering from the torment her body had just been through and the stress of their hasty escape. Her face was etched with worry as she cast a quick glance over her shoulder to see the ship heading out to sea, no boats launched.

They had no idea where they were or what sympathies the islanders might have. They had seemed hesitant to get involved back on the beach. Perhaps they were merely afraid of the Japanese. Perhaps they took no side at all. Greg and Amanda proceeded through the village under the watchful—and perhaps scornful—eyes of everyone they passed. They were exhausted, of course, but so much more than that. They were free.

Greg led Amanda down a narrow street and into an alley that cut between that road and what seemed to be the main thoroughfare. The houses there were little more than huts; some of the more impressive ones were constructed of reclaimed boards and bits of rough-hewn pine. The roofs in all cases were thatch. He knew what a sight they must be, two white-skinned, drenched people running through the little village. There was no way to be casual about it.

One more turn and they were in another alley, between two rows of little houses and safe from prying eyes. Not even a single window opened onto the alley, only a lone back door that had been nailed shut. Greg pulled Amanda to a stop, leaning abruptly against the wall and grabbing onto her.

"We made it. By God, we're free!" He laughed then and kissed her, spinning her around with the last bit of energy he had left in him.

"Yes, we are. Free. Oh my God! I can't believe we did that." She was laughing now too, great gales of near-hysterical laughter pealing across the town. "They didn't come after us."

"And it took so long for them to realize we'd gone . . . it all seems so surreal."

"Greg, what if they didn't come after us because they know something we don't."

He searched her eyes, knitted his brow. "Like what?"

"I don't know. Like maybe they'll come back later. Or they know the natives will capture us for them and turn us in. Or . . . something."

"Well, I think we'd be fools to stay in the last place they saw us. We should find a way out of here." Greg looked about him, eyes filled with worry. "I wonder where 'here' is."

Amanda was about to say something when a man appeared at the head of the alley. He was tall and quite thin. He wore khakis and a checked shirt and his shoes were covered with dust. But his demeanor was formal and his eyes shone and as soon as he spoke, her fears were dispelled.

"Here is Pangasang. Just outside Isabela City." His accent was British, his smile genuine. He stepped forward with his hand outstretched. "My name is Reginald Whitehouse. People around here call me Reggie."

Greg moved forward tentatively but he shook Reggie's hand.

"I'm Greg and this is Amanda. Is there a base around here? How is it that you're here?"

"No, there's no base here. At least no formal military base. Some have come and gone and the island changes hands bi-weekly. But all is well, really." He looked Amanda up and down, his smile widening and making her uncomfortable. "And you, Amanda, are not from around here."

"That's obvious, I suppose, from the color of my skin."

"And your designer jeans." He chuckled and reached into his pocket for a cigar. "What I mean is, when are you from?"

Amanda shot a look of confusion and terror at Greg, who put his arm around her and drew her near. "I'm afraid I don't take your meaning," Greg answered.

Reggie waved a hand in the air and smiled. "No matter. You two must be hungry. Why don't you come back to my house. We can have a nice lunch and then see about getting you back onto American soil, eh?"

CHAPTER TWELVE

They decided to follow him if for no other reason than to find out what he knew about the time anomaly. He seemed harmless enough, if not a bit eccentric. His house was a short distance away, and they crossed the road and walked through the small town, Reggie nodding here and there as people greeted him. It was obvious that he had been here for quite a while. They all seemed to know him.

Reggie's house was not what they had expected. In contrast to the huts and lean-tos scattered about the island, his home was made of brick and had a clay tile roof. It was charming in a sort of rustic way. Amanda noticed that a picture of the Queen graced the hallway wall.

Inside, it was cool and homey. Antiques stood next to homemade items; some of the bric-a-brac was out of place there. Amanda took it all in, her eyes wide and her mind trying to wrap itself around the most recent events. What had he meant when he'd asked her 'when are you from'?"

"Reggie? Is that you?" The accent was native rather than British and when the woman attached to it came around the corner, she was pure ebony grace. She moved like a titled woman from ages past and her clothes were clearly custom tailored. She smiled graciously and bowed a bit, a tribute to her heritage. "I did not know you'd brought guests, dear."

"And this is the reason I am still here," said Reggie, his face lighting up as he stooped to kiss his much shorter wife. "This is my wife, Maleah. My dear, I came across these two good people just as they escaped from a Japanese ship bound, no doubt, for the nearest prisoner of war camp."

"Oh my dear," she said, shaking her head. "You were lucky to get away. You must be hungry. Come. I have prepared lunch for Reggie and there is enough for all."

They followed her down the short hall to a very well-appointed kitchen. The table was set for two, but Maleah quickly corrected this. Something smelled wonderful and Amanda found herself drooling as she sat down. She felt awkward and dazed. Reggie set her nerves on edge.

"Now, as we eat, I want you to tell me the story of Greg and Amanda," Reggie began, his face still bright and happy.

"There's not much to tell," Greg began cautiously. He shot a look at Amanda, then leaned back in his chair.

"Oh, come now. Please do not try to put one over on me." He paused to check their faces and then continued. "Amanda wears designer jeans from at least the nineties. And I'm willing to bet she's owned a cell phone or two in her time. How do I know this?" He paused to laugh, an act which drew a glare of derision from Maleah. "I know this because I was born in 1946."

Amanda gasped a bit, shook the cobwebs out of her head while Maleah delivered their plates. "But that isn't for two more years," Amanda said snidely.

"Marvelous, isn't it?" He laughed again, then tore a piece from the large roll on his plate. "I came through a sort of time portal and ended up here five years ago. But you already know that. You came through it too."

She looked at Greg again, her face paling. "I . . . we were stranded on an island and that's where the Japanese captured us."

"Do tell." He sounded excited, joyous. "Was that before or after you came through the portal. Now, don't try to fool me. I know all of it. Why do you think I have a picture of the Queen of England, taken in 1984?"

Amanda's shoulders drooped and she stared at her plate. "Greg didn't come through the portal. Only I did. The boat I was on at the time was destroyed and we ended up beached on that island. The Japanese really did find us there. But I've no idea how to get back home."

Reggie's face had softened; his eyes had lost a bit of their sparkle. "My dear Amanda, I'm so sorry. I have to tell you that the portal is extremely finicky as to when and how it shows up." He shot a glance at Maleah. It made him sad, Amanda thought. "I came back here from 1984. I was out on a fishing trip when we ran into that thing. My boat, too, was destroyed and of my five friends, I was the only one who survived."

"I found him washed up on the beach one morning when I went to do laundry. I was only sixteen, but I got my brothers to help me drag him to our home. We cared for him and nursed him back to health." Maleah smiled and patted Reggie's hand. "And we've been together ever since."

"Oh, don't get the wrong idea," Reggie grumbled. "I would never. But I waited around for her to come of age. I knew the moment that my eyes locked upon hers that we were meant to be together forever. And I waited for two years for her to come of age so that we could be married. In the meantime, knowing what I know about the war and the future, I made my fortune."

"You interfered." Greg's tone was accusatory, gruff. "You changed things."

"I changed nothing significant. Why do you think we stay here? We're hiding. We can't let anyone know where I came from nor what I know. So we stay here on this little island. I don't need any identification. I don't need a job. Nobody asks any questions and we are quite safe."

"I can't believe we've found someone else who knows about that thing." Amanda smiled sheepishly at Reggie. "I was beginning to think I'd merely gone mad."

Greg picked up his fork, poked his food for a bit, then shoveled a huge pile of beans and rice into his mouth. He sighed with joy and closed his eyes for a moment. "Maleah, you are a wonderful cook." He swallowed hard and looked at Reggie. "It's my fault that Amanda's here."

"It's not," Amanda objected, putting her hand on his arm and squeezing it a bit.

"It is. My plane was hit out over the ocean. I was going down and sent out an SOS call. Through some weird trick of that time portal, the signal reached Amanda's ham radio some seventy years in the future. She came to rescue me. If not for that, she would be safely at home right now."

"And I'd still be miserable and alone. Don't you dare blame yourself, Greg." She finally took a bite of her food, finding it every bit as enchanting and delicious as Greg had. "I don't suppose you have any idea how that thing works? Have you seen it since?"

Reggie shook his head and looked mournful. "I have no idea how it works. But I have seen it. It shows up randomly, almost always during a storm. I think it has something to do with the lightning, the water, and the temperature. I've never seen it when it's cold. And I've never seen it on land."

"Well, that proves my theory, then." Amanda looked pleased with herself, though only for a moment. "I don't suppose you know how it works. I mean, do I have to be in the same boat, the same number of people . . ."

"You mean, can Greg go back with you? I don't know. From what I know of theoretical physics, there should be no matter-mass requirement. So long as you don't meet your past self or come in contact in any way, you should be fine."

Suddenly, Greg perked up, sitting straight and narrowing his eyes. "You've been back to your time. I know you have. How else would you have that damned picture of the Queen?"

"My good man, have you ever been on a British vessel? I think not. Otherwise, you would know that virtually every one large enough to bear it, has a picture of her majesty on board. The painting came with me. It was one of the few items I managed to salvage and restore from the wreck of the boat."

"I'm sorry. I just . . ."

"Quite all right, chap. I can understand how unsettling this entire experience must have been for you. Really I do. It's a bloody nightmare, I'll say." He smiled, looking more relaxed again, more confident. "So, do you both intend to go into the portal?"

"We do, yes." Greg took Amanda's hand and gave it a squeeze. "If we can find it again."

"I see. Why not just stay here? It would be safer that way. Hunker down somewhere safe until the war ends in two years. Then you'll be free as birds."

"The temptation to change things is too strong. We might do something that alters the entire course of history."

"Such as reveal where Hitler is and when? I do understand, dear lady. It's almost overwhelming, isn't it?" Reggie had that smile down to a science. It was beginning to be a most disconcerting thing.

"Yes. Not to mention the bomb." Amanda nodded and frowned. "Besides, I can't bear to leave Greg."

"Then stay. It's quite pleasant here, really." He watched their faces, realizing that they would have none of it. "Very well. We shall try to get you back through that bloody portal then. Maleah, is there dessert?"

"Pear fritters, my love." Maleah stood with a smile and headed for the cupboard.

Reggie watched her as she walked, her hips swaying of their own accord, the way she carried herself. He smiled to himself. He was a very lucky man. "You haven't lived until you've tasted Maleah's pear fritters."

"Perhaps I'm missing something but how do we know we'll return to the right time, even if we get through the portal?" Greg let it sink in for a moment, then pressed on. "Amanda came from 2012. You came from 1984. What determines the time frame that lies beyond the portal?"

"That's a good question, young man. And I do wish I had an answer for you." He watched as Maleah set a bowl of fresh fritters on the table; took two of them for himself. "Perhaps it has to do with the location. I was just off the coast of Ireland when I got caught in it. It took me back to 1938. You were . . . where?"

Amanda swallowed a mouthful of fritters and coughed. "I was just off the coast of Maine. I went back to 1943."

"By God! That's it!" Reggie dusted off his hands and stood up, nearly toppling his chair in the process. He nearly ran from the room, his face alight with agitation and excitement. When he returned, he had a map in one hand. He unfurled it, letting it flow over the table, covering everything. "I was at about 15 degrees Longitude. You were at . . . let me see . . . about 65 degrees Longitude. As I live and breathe! You move one year for each ten degrees in Longitude." He sat down, folding his hands in his lap.

"So, to go back to 2012, I have to be at . . . that can't work. There are only 360 degrees of Longitude." Amanda blinked at him, screwed up her face in thought. "There aren't enough Longitude lines for that many years. Could it have something to do with the Latitude? The coordinates?"

Reggie rubbed his chin and thought for a moment. "If only we had more data. We can't derive a system from just two sets of coordinates."

Greg placed one hand gently on Amanda's arm and leaned forward. "If we have no way of knowing what year we'll end up in, then how can we do this?"

Her eyes met his and she paled. "I'm afraid you might be right."

"Unless my original theory holds true." Reggie looked very pleased with himself just then, his cockeyed smile sitting high on his face and his eyes glimmering in the light. "I believe that this field, this portal or whatever it is, is merely a two-way door. It exists between only two years at any one time, and that's why, if you had waited five minutes, gone into it later, you still would have come to 1943. For what it's worth, I strongly believe that you can only enter one specific portal. It will be visible only to you. And you can only go back to the time from which you came."

"But we can't be sure." Greg looked at him quite directly. There was a hint of fear in his eyes.

"No, we can't be sure. But if you want to try. I can get you there."

Amanda nodded emphatically. Greg looked at her, stunned. "Are you sure?" he asked sadly.

"Aren't you? We can be together, in the future. It's a much better world than this one."

"She's not wrong about that. I think you'll like it, Greg." Reggie smiled and it softened his face.

"All right," Greg said, throwing up his hands and slamming his back against the chair. "We'll go to 2012."

"Well, then, you shall spend the night with us. And tomorrow morning, I will take you in my boat to the northern point of the island. From there, you can look out over the horizon at the Sulu Sea and the Moro Gulf. It will give you the highest probability of spotting the thing."

"And when we do?" Greg looked askance at Reggie, already resigned to his fate as time traveler.

"Then, young man, you and your girl drive that pretty boat of mine straight into it."

Greg and Amanda spent the afternoon on the beach. They had missed the sun and the surf, the feel of sand between their toes. Conversation was brief and awkward; neither knew what to say to the other. The tension was a chasm between them; silence offered relief.

Hand in hand, they walked along the sand, still dripping from their latest swim. Amanda looked up suddenly, searching Greg's handsome face. It was creased with worry, aged from the ordeal they had suffered. "Am I being selfish?" she asked softly. "Be honest."

Greg stopped walking, turned his head to give her a sideways glance. "Not selfish, exactly. Foolish perhaps."

"Foolish?" It hurt. She knew it was honest and probably more than a little true. It hurt just the same.

"Yes." He turned to face her, his hands rubbing her arms, his eyes falling into hers. "We know we can be together here. We know where and when we are. But if we go through that portal or whatever it is, we don't know where we'll end up. Or if we'll survive it."

"If you stay here, what will happen? Will you go back to your unit? Continue to fight? Maybe be killed?" Tears threatened to spill onto her cheeks and her throat suddenly hurt.

"That's probably what will happen." He thought for a moment. "Or perhaps I could hide out here, with you, until the war ends. But that would make me a coward. I don't think you could love a coward. And I couldn't live with myself."

"So, if you go back and fight, what happens to me? They send me stateside. I won't see you for years. I have no friends, no family, no job, no money . . ."

"You can stay with my family."

She sighed heavily, frowned. "Until and unless you're killed in the war. Then what? If we go back to my time, we can live in my house, I have a job, at least some friends. There's no war for you to fight. We'll both be safe."

"And I won't exist. On paper, I don't exist. I'll be a serial number in the Navy files. A pilot who was shot down. Missing in action, considered dead for some seventy years."

"What it comes down to," she said reverently, "is that one of us has to give up our life to stay with the other." She thought she would cry just then, but a sudden thought occurred to her and she smiled. "There's only one fair way to solve this."

"What's that?"

"We flip a coin."

He smiled back. "I don't have a coin."

"Me either. Race you to the house."

They ran, kicking up clouds of sand with each step, laughing as they jockeyed for position. When they reached the back porch, Greg in the lead, Amanda stumbled and cried out, holding her lame left leg. Greg, ever the gentleman, hurried back to help her.

"Are you all right? Does it hurt?" He bent to examine the injured limb.

"Only when I laugh," she bellowed, shoving him to the ground and running away, peals of laughter ringing through the air as she hurried up the steps and into the house.

She was panting, her head swimming and her legs throbbing as she appeared in the kitchen. Maleah looked stunned, her face caught in a wide-eyed stare of confusion.

"Are you all right, Amanda?"

"Fine," she gasped. Behind her, the door opened and Greg stepped inside. "We just ran from the beach."

"You cheat!" Greg panted, holding his side and panting.

"Call it strategic humor," Amanda giggled. "Maleah, would you happen to have a coin we could borrow?"

"A coin? What kind of coin?" Maleah was confused but a smile teased at her lips.

"Any kind," Greg offered, dropping into a chair. "I call heads. Heads and we stay here."

"Tails and we go into the portal." Amanda dropped into the chair next to Greg's and hugged him. "Maleah, you flip it so that it's fair."

Maleah nodded, tossing the coin into the air, eyes following it as it landed in her hand and she flipped it over to the back of the other hand. "Are you sure?" she asked before revealing the coin.

They nodded, shared a quick kiss.

"It is tails." Maleah took her hand away, proffering the coin for their inspection.

"That's it, then. We go into the portal." He drew her close, hugging her and stroking her hair. "And live happily ever after."

Amanda helped Maleah prepare dinner that night. After nothing but fish, clams, crabs and fruits, everything they ate seemed like a feast. Maleah was a good cook and she was filled with wonderful stories of her childhood on the island that was her home. Amanda found that the more she listened to Maleah, the more nostalgic she became for their own little island home. She found that she longed for it. Would it really be so bad to just go back there, live the rest of their lives nestled in each other's arms, with no jobs, no pressure, no bills, no house, no children, no marriage, no friends. . . .

Yes, she decided. It would.

Together, the women served dinner. Conversation was light and jovial, though the backbeat of tension was constant. They retired early, grateful for their first night in a bed. It was a down mattress, old but soft and welcoming. It devoured them as they sank into it, creating a center rut as they gravitated toward each other. Blankets snugged up under their chins, they clung to each other, bodies entwined as he kissed her.

As always, she melted into his embrace. His touches were fire; his kisses were grace. She had never felt anything like what Greg made her feel; not even with Scott. They truly became one. She felt alive for the first time.

Reggie knocked on their door just after dawn. He apologized for waking them so early, but explained that the trip was long. He wanted to arrive before dark, then leave the next morning to return home.

Amanda and Greg shared a shower. It was hot and delicious. They'd had no idea how much they'd missed the simple things like showers and soap, soft towels and toothpaste. No matter what they were facing, it all made them feel lighter. Maleah's wonderful breakfast made them sigh with joy.

They went ahead to the boat, letting Reggie and Maleah have their time alone to say goodbye. Reggie was sacrificing a lot for them. It was a debt they could never pay back. To ease her mind about his sacrifice for them, Amanda told him three huge stocks to buy and when to buy them.

"You'll be rich beyond belief," she told him as they stood on the dock.

"We can't thank you enough for everything you've done," Greg added, shaking Reggie's hand and smiling. "I don't know what we'd have done without your help."

"Merely a little assist from one time traveler to another," he chuckled. "It was my pleasure. Safe journey, my friends. Be happy."

They watched him go, smiling and holding hands as they stood on the dock. He would drive home with Maleah, who had followed them up the coast in her Jeep. Amanda and Greg would wait . . . and watch.

The boat was a beauty. A thirty-foot Chris-Craft, it had every amenity imaginable. They had no idea how long they might have to wait, or even if the anomaly would show up. But Reggie had packed the boat full of food and there was a utility hook-up at the marina, where Reggie had paid for three months in advance.

"If it doesn't show up within three months," Amanda had said, something itching at the back of her mind, "I think we should give up. We can't live our entire lives sitting around and waiting for something that might never happen. We need to live."

During the day, they sat on deck in the shade of the bimini and watched. They weren't sure it would appear during the day, or if they would see it if it did. They watched just the same. At night, they took six-hour shifts.

For a week they watched, until they thought they would go insane from inactivity. Even on the island they had had freedom of movement and activities to keep them from going stir-crazy. It was almost like being back on the Japanese ship again, trapped in that awful dank cell for most of the day.

On the eighth night, Greg took Amanda's place for the early watch. She had been feeling unwell all day, her head achy and her muscles sore. So, he took her shift, letting her go to bed early. He sat on the bow, just over the A-berth which they shared each night. His hands were cupped around a warm coffee mug and he scanned the horizon every few minutes, looking for that tell-tale wall of light.

The harbor was dark as could be. There was no land in the visible area of the ocean, no ships crossing the pitch. Even the slight illumination from a boat's running lights could easily be seen, so

Greg knew that he would spot the anomaly the minute it appeared. For the moment at least, there was nothing.

At three in the morning, just as he was about to wake Amanda for her watch, Greg spotted a bright spot on the horizon. It appeared suddenly, just as his eyes made one last sweep of the ocean. At first, it was just a lighter shade of darkness but the light grew by the second, becoming something irrefutably tangible and moving across his line of sight.

"Amanda!" he called, rising from the bow, knocking as he stood. "Amanda, come quick."

She stumbled up the stairs, eyes still blurry with sleep. She yawned and swiped at them as she came onto the deck, the chill night air doing more to awaken her than anything else. "What is it?"

"Look!" Greg said, thrusting out his arm.

She followed his arm to the end, spotting the wall of light which drifted across the horizon. "My God! That's it."

She was off like a shot, hurrying to the pilot house and firing up the engine. Her heart was hammering, her breath stinted and painful. "Cast off the lines," she called back to him. "Hurry."

"Already done." He was at her back, hands on her shoulders.

"Then away we go. You ready?"

"Ready as I'll ever be."

She put the boat in gear, increased the throttle just enough to get them away from the dock, then sped up as fast as she could without flooding the motor. "Whatever happens, Greg, know that I love you with all my heart."

"I love you, too, Frank. Always." He kissed her, briefly.

The wall was moving across the ocean, not toward the land. Amanda pushed the throttle, kicked the boat into high gear. The boat bounced on the waves, its bow cutting through the water, leaving a wide and vicious wake behind it. They were catching up, but slowly.

"I've got the throttle wide open. She won't go any faster."

"I hope we catch it before it goes away." Greg had to admit to more than a little fear pounding at his temples. His hands gripped the top rail as hard as they could, knuckles white and his eyes wide.

The portal loomed ahead of them some two miles. Amanda cursed the boat, the engine, the slowness of their progress. As they came within one mile, she brought the boat around slightly, wanting to hit the portal head on and not at an angle. She remembered all too well the sensation of going through that portal, the fear of being swept backward, her impact with the aft rail.

"Hold on. It will try to sweep you backward, pull at you. Don't let it take you off the back of the boat or you'll be lost."

Greg nodded, dry-swallowed. "Okay."

For the first time, Amanda got a good look at the thing. It went up hundreds of feet, beyond the point where she could see. The lights inside swirled, almost as though they were alive. And as they drew nearer to it, the air became warmer, until it was as hot as a desert day. The hairs on her arms stood on end and she felt her scalp prickle with cast-off electricity.

"Here we go," she hollered, shoving the throttle one last little bit forward.

The boat bucked beneath them, speeding slightly, giving its all. Greg tightened his grip on the rail, his entire body tensing, prepared for the worst.

The bow of the boat disappeared and Amanda gasped as she realized what was about to happen. The boat, heading the opposite direction as the portal, slowed as it entered the light. Amanda felt her own actions slowed, including her heart which had been pounding a fast beat in her chest. The lights were almost upon them now. She couldn't see the bow of the boat, or the vent over their forward bed. The sound of the motor was diffused in the thick air, then went away altogether.

"Hold on tight," she called to Greg as the force of it dragged at her, pulling her backward, threatening to separate her from the boat. For a moment, she felt her feet leave the deck. Then she forced them back down.

The light was fully on her then, the swirling sensation making her dizzy and nauseous. There was no going back, nothing she could do to hurry or stop their progress through the anomaly. She turned. Greg was struggling to hold on.

His hands gripped the rail in white-knuckled desperation. His face, so handsome, so soft, was a study in pain and fear. His feet had been swept off the deck. His grip on the rail was all that tethered him to her. He was slipping.

The lights were amidships; she could once more see the bow. Still, Greg was losing his grip. It was pulling him backward, off the boat.

Frantic, she braced herself on the pilot's seat and grabbed onto his arms. The force pulled at her too, compressing the seat back and crushing the breath from her. Still, she held onto him.

"Greg, no!" she screamed as his hands slipped.

She caught one hand as it was pried free of the rail, held on for dear life. They just had to hang on until the wall passed over them. Then they would be safe. Her arms shook and she nearly collapsed as she looked into his face. It was strained and deeply rutted with the effort of holding onto her.

"Hold on!" she yelled, tightening her grip on his arm, feeling it pull harder and harder against her grasp. She was losing him.

He grabbed onto the seat, tried to get a good grip, but the pull was too strong.

"No. No!"

Her screams cut the air as the lights engulfed the boat. The bow was not yet to the other side but the lights swirled around them. Greg was only barely holding on. Amanda gripped him tighter, pulling him toward her with every ounce of strength that she had. Her entire body shook with the effort, her heart sped until she thought it would burst.

"Hurry, hurry, hurry."

The bow cut through the lights, emerged on the other side, unscathed. As the portal gave birth to the boat, the force on it eased. In another minute, the lights would be past where Amanda and Greg stood, clinging desperately to each other.

The anomaly pushed itself over top of her, easing her strain, letting gravity and the forward pull ease for her. But it still pulled at Greg, pulled at him as though it didn't want to let go. It was a living thing now, intelligent, and completely unwilling to let Greg pass through.

Greg screamed, loud and long, grasping desperately with his right hand, trying to find purchase. Amanda screamed along with him, grabbing at him, her mind splitting with the possibility that she could lose him.

And then it dawned on her: Just let go. Let go of the boat, let go of the future, let go of your home. Stay with Greg. Hold onto him and stay with him and love him.

She scrambled over the top of the seat, launching herself at him, grabbing onto him with arms and legs and holding for dear life. If the future wouldn't have him, she wouldn't have it. She would let the lights and the pull rip her off the stern of the boat, leave her in the past with Greg.

But it didn't.

It wouldn't.

They bounced onto the deck, a tangle of frantically clinging limbs, grimaces of fear and exhaustion. They bounced and slid, colliding with the stern of the boat in a huge pile of bruised flesh. Amanda cried out and wrapped her arms around Greg. The lights were on top of them still, the darkness creeping along the length of the boat, nearly to them, pushing them.

"I can't get through," he said, agonized.

"I'll stay," she answered. "Just hold onto me tight and wherever you go, I go too."

They lay on the deck, pressed hard against the aft section, the lights marching toward them without regard for their torment. Eyes closed, Amanda held tight, rolling so that she was between Greg and the wood. To take him, the anomaly would have to press him straight through her.

It was almost over. No matter the outcome, they were going to end up together. Past or future, it didn't matter.

The boat ceased forward movement, seemed to stand still in the moment, hung in the air. And then it dropped, bucked forward as the lights washed over Greg, taking him into their grasp and slamming him against her, her against the stern. Her head hit the wood, bringing stars to her field of vision, and then the lights were just . . . gone.

Amanda was alone in the boat.

CHAPTER THIRTEEN

Amanda called for him for over an hour, finally collapsing upon the boat's deck in a fit of tears and exhaustion. She had turned to leap into the water, but by the time her legs got her into a standing position, the lights had gone. They had passed over her and winked out, as though they had never been there. They hadn't wanted her back. They hadn't let Greg pass.

She had no idea how long she had lain there crying, but by the time her tears dried and she had opened her eyes, the sun was coming up. There was no way for her to know where she was or when she was. She had no idea of which direction to go.

They had seen the lights from where they were moored; she had seen the lights of the city right before the lights had surrounded her. If she had not moved in location, she should be able to see the city. She could not.

The boat had half a tank of fuel and enough food and water left for five days. At that moment, she wasn't sure she wanted to live; considered just leaping into the ocean and letting it take her. Or perhaps she should just stay where she was and pray that the anomaly came back for her. There was no good way out of this.

She sat up, looking at the water, making sure that Greg wasn't floating nearby. She could see nothing but waves and sky, the occasional fin of a large fish. He was gone and there was no way to get him back.

Several hours later, as the sun was nearing its highest point, a boat approached her. She knew from the orange markings that it was a Coast Guard boat. It looked new, modern. She was truly home. She stood to greet them, waving limply and trying to smile as they pulled alongside.

"Do you need assistance, ma'am?" asked the nice young man at the side.

"I seem to be lost. I don't suppose you know where I am?" They would never believe the truth.

"You're about ten miles out from Tenant's Harbor."

She nodded. "What day is it?"

"How long have you been out here, ma'am?" His face had a look of suspicion.

"That's why I asked what day it is. The exact date, please?"

"It's July 21, 2012. Are you all right? Are you injured?"

"I'm fine. If it's okay, I'll follow you back in, okay?"

She tried to seem sane, collected. But her brain was screaming and her heart was broken. She had been gone for over two months by her time. She had gone out in another boat, a single, lonely girl on a rescue mission. She had come home in this boat, one half of a couple, the other half lost. She turned toward the wheel, firing up the boat. As she pulled away, the tears began to fall.

The very nice Coast Guard officer made sure she was safely tied onto her dock, then bid her a speedy goodbye. Something about her demeanor had unnerved them all. Heck, she even unnerved herself.

As she made her way back to the house, she wondered how she was going to pick up her old life here. She had known love, had been the second part of a beautiful couple. She had been happy. The house, the job, the people in her life were all still the same. She was not.

Once she had gotten a shower, checked her messages (there were dozens) and grabbed something to eat, she settled down to repair what had been broken. She called Dana first, knowing that she would be upset if she weren't at the top of the list.

"Hello," called her happy, sing-song voice.

"It's me. Amanda." Her voice was soft and pained. The sadness wouldn't let go of her.

"Oh my God! Amanda! Where are you? What's happened? Are you all right?"

She smiled at the rapid-fire interrogation. It was so Dana. "I'm fine. I'm at home. But this story has to be told in person. If at all."

"On my way. I'll bring wine and Chinese food." A long pause and then, "God, you had me so scared."

"I love you too, girl. See you soon."

She hung up, staring off into space for a moment, wondering how upset her boss was and whether she had a job left or not. She dialed his office number and bit into her lip, waiting for his voice to growl in her ear.

"Hi, Mr. Haines. It's Amanda."

"Amanda," he answered flatly. "Where have you been?"

"Actually, Mr. Haines, I was lost at sea." She swallowed, waited for the yelling, the accusations. There was none. "I heard a distress call over my ham radio, and went out to rescue them. But my boat broke down."

"And you were stuck out there for nearly two months?"

"Yes, unfortunately. I understand if you've replaced me . . ."

"Of course I replaced you, Amanda," he said sharply, taking a long pause before he spoke again. "With a temp. Amanda, you've worked for me for a long time. You're not the type to shirk responsibility. I knew something must have happened. So, if you're back on your feet, you can start back at work day after tomorrow."

"Oh, thank you, Mr. Haines. Thank you so much for having faith in me."

"No problem, Amanda. See you in two days."

She began to cry softly then. A lot of things would have to be fixed . . . but at least she still had the wherewithal to fix them. The doorbell rang then, and Dana peered through the sidelights, waving with one finger. She had a bottle of wine in one hand and a bag from Mr. Cho's in the other. Amanda let her in.

"Oh my God! I'm so glad you're okay." Dana flew in to hug Amanda, the wine striking her sore back and the scent of Chinese food engulfing her. "You sure had me scared."

Amanda closed the door and walked Dana to the dining room. "I have one hell of a story to tell you. I hope you've got some time."

"For my bestie? You betcha!" She dropped into the chair and tore open the bag. "Now, start from the beginning and don't leave out a single detail."

The wine was drunk and the food eaten and over the course of two hours, Amanda imparted her whole sad story to Dana. Sometimes laughing, sometimes crying, she gave her every juicy detail, knowing how insane it all sounded. When she had finished, Dana sat back and smiled, cocking her head to one side like some particularly slow dog.

"So, you went out in your boat to save that guy and you hit your head. How long were you lying there in that boat?"

Amanda gawped. Her jaw hung like a loose fender. "Didn't you hear a word I said?"

"I did," answered Dana, patting her hand. "And it was a lovely hallucination. But you're home now. Everything's fine."

Amanda sighed and let her head droop. "It was real. The whole thing, Dana. It really happened."

Dana leaned forward, smiling patronizingly and sighing. "I know it seemed real, honey. But it was just a result of your head injury. Maybe you should see a doctor."

Amanda blinked at her, shook her head. "I'm fine. But I am exhausted. I think I'm going to go to bed."

Dana showed herself out and Amanda locked the door. No one would ever believe her story. How could they? Even she realized how ludicrous it all sounded.

Amanda was exhausted, but before she could sleep, there was something she had to do. She went to her father's study and unlocked the door, slipping into the room and settling in his chair. The radio should still be tuned to the same channel that Greg's message had come in on. She switched on the equipment and waited for it to warm up. Then she listened. She listened all night. She heard nothing.

She reasoned that the signal had only come through because of the storm, so she abandoned the radio on the third night. She had returned to her job, fixed all her bills. Everything was back to normal. Everything but her.

Every single night, she sat on the deck of the boat, watching the ocean for signs of the anomaly. When it stormed, she parked herself in front of the radio, listening for word from the past. If she could just get a single message through, she could let Greg know that she was safe and that she hadn't forgotten him. If she could find another portal, she could get back to him.

For months, she watched and listened and not one sign of the past seeped into her world. For the rest of her life, she would watch and listen, searching for Greg, praying to be allowed to return to him. She would never love anyone else. The universe had given her a single chance at happiness and she had blown it.

That fall, there was a horrible storm. The sky was alight with constant flashes of lightning and the ground shook with the force of the thunder. Amanda had listened to the radio until the power went out. Then she had watched through the back window for the portal to appear. It never showed.

One evening after work, she went into the study - which she no longer kept locked—and turned on the radio. It crackled and popped, but the lights came on. Suddenly, there was a particularly loud pop and the lights all went out on the radio. She screamed and cursed at it, slapped the side of it with her hand. Then she sank into the chair in a fit of tears, miserable.

After bemoaning her constant failure for nearly an hour, she decided to take the case off the radio to see if there was anything obvious wrong with it. A tube had blown, its broken top having scattered small shards of glass all over the inside of the radio. She dumped them out over the trash can, then took care to remove the remains of the broken tube. Perhaps she could get another one, fix the radio.

The next afternoon, when work was over, she went to an electronics store downtown. The ad in the phonebook had declared, "In business since 1947." Surely they must have what she needed. Armed with the broken tube and the make and model number of her radio, she pulled into the only parking space near the store and walked a block. The store was definitely old, the bricks fighting back moss and the sidewalk before it cracked with age. A tarnished old bell tinkled at her as she pulled open the door. Inside, the air was warm and still. It smelled of plastic and dust.

"How can I help you," asked the man behind the counter. He was maybe twenty-five and bright eyed. He had a ready smile.

"I have an old radio," she began, "that belonged to my father. This tube blew last night and I was hoping to get a replacement." She held out the broken piece, wrapped in a paper towel.

The young man took it from her, squinting at the tiny numbers on the metal base. "I think I have a few of these in the back. I'll go see."

He swept aside the curtain that separated the front of the store from the back, but was stopped in his tracks by an elderly man. His back was hunched and he walked with a cane. He had a full head of thick white hair and his blue eyes still shimmered.

"This is what you need," the old man said with a grin. "It'll fix you right up."

Amanda watched as he leaned on the counter, holding the tube out to her, still in its box. There was something in those wise old eyes, in the way he tilted his head each time he smiled. A chill ran up her back as she took the box, her finger brushing his for a mere second. "Thank you so much. I'm lost without my radio." She reached into her purse and placed a five-dollar-bill on the counter.

"It's a horrible thing . . . to be lost." He nodded. "Much better to be found."

She turned and headed for the door, her hand barely reaching the knob before he spoke to her again.

"Have a nice day . . . Frank."

ABOUT THE AUTHOR

Patricia Lee Macomber is the former editor-in-chief of *ChiZine*. She has been published in *Cemetery Dance* magazine and such anthologies as *Shadows Over Baker Street, Little Red Riding Hood In the Big Bad City,* and *Dark Arts*. Along with her husband, David Niall Wilson, she has written *An Unkindness of Ravens* and *Stargate Atlantis: Brimstone*. Her first solo release, *Zombie A Love Story,* is now available. Currently, she lives in North Carolina with her husband, David, and their children.

Rendezvous
PRESS

CROSSROAD
PRESS

www.ingramcontent.com/pod-product-compliance
Lightning Source LLC
Chambersburg PA
CBHW070835020826
48982CB00019B/1273/J

* 9 7 8 1 9 3 7 5 3 0 9 3 8 *